Ganges Boy

Archana Prasanna

NEW YORK
VIRGINIA

Ganges Boy
by Archana Prasanna

ISBN 9781938467387

Published by
köehlerbooks™
an imprint of Morgan James Publishing

5 Penn Plaza, 23rd floor
c/o Morgan James Publishing
New York, NY 10001
212-574-7939
www.koehlerbooks.com

Publisher
John Köehler

Executive Editor
Joe Coccaro

For My Parents

CHAPTER ONE

Kabir was a shy, awkward lad with shaggy hair and patched clothing that never quite fit. He assisted his mother, Sanskruti, as she worked at her loom in the sari factory that sat at the edge of his village just south of the great city Varanasi and close to the River Ganges. The villagers were easily characterized: impoverished and always hungry. It was the same for all of them. It had been the same for generations, an unbroken chain of poverty that now lingered into the twentieth century. They were the poorest of India's poor. Kabir had learned his place—somewhere nobody else would want to be.

Kabir often escaped from the mundane tasks of his life through wonder-filled daydreams in which he stared, bravely diving into the waters of the River Ganges from a great height, or racing with long, perfect strides along the ghats, receiving looks of admiration from all he passed.

His mother would gently bring him back to the important tasks at hand.

"Watch what you're doing! Keep the weft threads taut, or those rows will be crooked and Mr. Malik will be unhappy with us."

"Yes, Ma," he groaned impatiently though never disrespectfully.

He still managed guarded glances across the rows of looms in the big room and out the small, grimy windows in search of some pleasant diversion or promise of fun awaiting him outside once his day was finished.

Ten minutes earlier, his best friend, Omar, had flashed him a sign from across the room. They could get together later. For the time being, Kabir focused on the beater and battened the weave his mother had just finished. She had completed the border of the shawl she was working on and began the intricate design, which would render it in the popular Benares pattern. Of all the weavers, Kabir thought his mother was the best.

Sanskruti was a pleasant looking woman. Her long, agile, slender hands were perfect for creating delicate patterns with the fine, hand-dyed, colorful thread. She had long, thick black hair that was exaggerated by her flawless olive skin. A nose ring, the only piece of jewelry she owned, sparkled amidst her sweaty face in the factory. She worked long hours but despite the grueling work, her oval face always remained gentle and her eyes danced brightly. They were accentuated and enhanced by her modest use of black eyeliner. She spoke softly and frequently cast smiles in her son's direction, as if telling him their workday would soon come to an end. Kabir would usually acknowledge her with a nod or by returning the smile, imperceptible to many but never to a mother.

Kabir had been assisting his mother at the factory for most of his life, almost as long as she had worked there. Even so, she rarely allowed him to do any of the actual weaving or sewing. He was relegated to tasks such as carrying spools of yarn and battening the weft threads in the loom. He had other duties at the factory as well. Along with his friend Omar he spent some time every day dying the wool yarn and keeping the factory workstations supplied. The two of them looked for any opportunity to sneak into the vat rooms in the back, near a pond where they could dump the unusable, diluted dyes and mix new combinations of color. It became more than a pleasant diversion and regularly brought out the imp in each of them—the imp that universally resides somewhere deep inside every ten-year-old-boy.

Kabir was a lanky lad, with arms and legs that seemed to be too long for his torso. He grew out his thick, black scruffy hair to make his thin body look bigger. In actuality,

Kabir's muscles were more developed than most other boys because of the manual labor he performed in the factory. But because of his skinny stature, that always went unnoticed.

While working on the beater, Kabir smiled to himself. His colorfully stained hands reminded him of how Omar had dropped a stone into the mixture they were playfully brewing in the pond several days before, splashing him with indigo dye. They took delight in catching the other off guard and creating indelible splash marks on one another's clothing and skin. The very best, however, was a face stain, one ample enough to remain for a week or longer. They considered that the ultimate score on the other.

They had to be careful so it didn't appear they were messing around or wasting dye, because Mr. Malik, the factory manager, would strike them or dock Kabir's mother's pay if he suspected mischief. In cases of their more egregious infractions, Sanskruti would receive a slap as well, which was something the boys never wanted to risk.

Malik was a fat old man, generally disgusting in appearance, who had frown lines etched deeply in his forehead, disclosing his typical state of mind. His great size caused him to be perennially out of breath. Beads of sweat dripped from his face, his brow, his nose, even his ear-lobes. He was an inconsiderate sort with a quick temper. He had but one goal: to see that his workers spent every moment executing their tasks perfectly.

Kabir glanced in his mother's direction and relived a flash of remorse from an incident that happened several months earlier. Malik had mistakenly thought Kabir had broken a wooden shuttle that he discovered lying on a table near the door to the vat room. As was typical of the man and before really looking into the matter, he confronted Sanskruti and administered a series of stinging blows as punishment for her son's alleged carelessness.

Within moments, the manager of the loom room corrected Malik, disclosing that he was the one who had placed the shuttle there for repairs. It had broken through routine use, as they so often did. Malik would not apologize to Sanskruti or admit his error, of course. Kindness had no place in his approach to living.

The heartbreaking memory passed and Kabir again turned his attention to the windows, hoping to see Omar waiting outside.

"Ma," he whispered, "It will soon be the time. May I go to play first?"

She paused for a moment and looked into his beautiful, dark eyes. They pleaded for a break. Although she was as lenient as any mother in the factory, she was reluctant to allow him to go off with Omar, his Muslim friend, during the call to prayer. She broke a faint smile and returned to her work without a word. He understood it was her way of permitting him to leave without either approving of it or speaking it aloud.

Kabir quickly made his way across the factory floor, weaving his way among the other looms. He smiled at the women and children as he passed but didn't take time to stop and chat. They understood that a boy his age had to make the most of whatever time he got for himself.

The factory was nothing more than a dimly lit claustrophobic hut. Pieces of cloth and dirt circled the air. The ground was made of mud, and Kabir often distracted himself by digging his bare feet into the ground. There were six weaving looms, tightly packed together side by side, made from bamboo and logs. Each weaver was given a working station. The working station was almost like another home. Workers spent nearly twelve hours working on saris, with a short lunch break during prayer time. Many of the weavers gossiped while they performed their repetitive work. Sanskruti was rather shy. She had decorated her station with drawings and paintings that she had done and would look to these pictures when in need for a break. Amidst the flimsy looms, sweaty odors, and clattering sounds, beautiful colors and patterns took shape. Stacks of cloth would arrive monthly, which would stay in Malik's office under his supervision.

Malik watched over the toiling workers through the ever-soiled glass window of his ever-cluttered office near the front of the building. He became annoyed when someone arrived late or left early. His glistening brow furrowed as he watched Kabir exit through the open sliding door that led to the loading dock. He clearly wished he had some reason to keep the boy at work.

Outside, Kabir paused for a moment to inhale deeply, clearing his lungs of the continually polluted air inside the building. He had been breathing the chemical fumes from the factory since birth, but had never become used to them. The chemical fumes were exhaust from the dyes that would color the saris or threads.

All day long, every day of his life, his young lungs struggled. He greeted the fresh air with a smile and almost immediately found renewed energy building within his being.

As he looked toward the docks, hoping to locate Omar, he caught sight of his friend's tunic as it disappeared behind the factory. He ran toward the river and searched for him among the crates and pallets. Omar was on the dock at the river. They spotted each other at the same moment and met at the dock. Before they could agree on how to spend the small amount of time they had, the call to prayer split the air bringing their plans to a screeching halt.

Kabir and his mother were, more or less, Hindu, but lived in a Muslim neighborhood. She had settled there before he was born, and it had become home. Despite Kabir's love for the village, he often felt isolated because of the ridicule from other children. Muslim children taunted him for his looks and for wearing stained, patched clothing.

Truly, he was never fully accepted into the community. His father had practiced Islam and his mother, Hinduism. Kabir never viewed the religions as different. It didn't matter that Muslims prayed to Allah and Hindus to various deities. Kabir found comfort in both and overlooked any differences.

Kabir, having been born out of wedlock, was seen as nothing more than a bastard child unworthy of respect or of worshiping any god.

"Alla-a-a-ahu Akbar ...," a voice wailed through the village, crackling over an aging public address system from the mosque. The two boys instinctively turned their heads toward its source. Omar smiled and began walking. Kabir matched his quickening pace. Malik exited the factory to make his way to salat as well. He watched them ahead of him, laughing and talking back and forth as they broke into a trot. He shook his head in disgust, knowing that Kabir would again be present at the holy masjid.

After arriving at the mosque, Omar found a spare mat leaning against an ancient stone wall. The boys entered the open-air prayer hall through the archway and navigated through the small sea of prostrate men. Omar found an area in the courtyard free from stones fallen from the crumbling walls and unfurled his mat so he would be facing the mihrab where the imam was already leading the prayer. He hurried to prostrate himself and took up the chant with the others.

Brushing aside pebbles and other debris, Kabir made a seat on one of the larger fallen stones and watched the imam respectfully. He tried to ignore the sneers from several children, but his face went red with embarrassment and he forced himself to hold back tears. Even this place of worship was not free from the taunts that seemed to await him everywhere.

Malik rolled out his sajada, a portable work of art, plush and ornate. It was one of the finest in the region. As he knelt, his eyes met those of Mullah Najid, who had looked up momentarily as he saw the boys arrive. The Mullah's glare telegraphed culpability, and Malik tensed at the thought of unofficial reprisals. He shook his head and positioned his palms upward as if to signal disapproval of Kabir's presence and his powerlessness to keep the mosque undefiled, even though the boy worked at his factory. It was, he believed, a problem under the purview of the mosque officials, and he certainly had no authority to say who could enter its confines to praise Allah. The Mullah lowered his head and continued his prayer.

Kabir sat quietly on his chalky stone perch, watching the imam as he prayed. He fiddled with a Shiva lingam in his pocket, trying to make sure no one discovered he had brought a Hindu deity into a Muslim mosque. He inadvertently kicked one of the rolled mats, causing it to fall against a lady who was walking by.

"What a strange boy," the lady remarked in disapproval

as she moved on.

Though such remarks were not unfamiliar to him, it still seemed odd that his slightest indiscriminate act should attract such notice and ridicule. One of his life's lessons had been that acts of prejudice need little—often, no—provocation. He thought it was disturbing that the last remark out of a person's mouth before prayer would be one of contempt. It stirred in him questions about religion and relationships.

He surveyed the courtyard, stopping to look at what was left of the now fallen, but once grand, minaret. He imagined that it had originally risen to a height of thirty feet. It was difficult to tell. Most things in and around his village, including the courtyard, had looked the same his entire life. He had passed by it often with his father, who had explained that old traditions needed to be preserved. It was the main reason Kabir liked going there with Omar for the midday prayer—the comfort of tradition. His father had never taken him, but promised that he would when he came of age. With his father's death the previous year, that dream had died as well.

It began months before, when Kabir followed Omar to prayer one day. It seemed somehow comfortable, and he decided to keep going. He felt a kinship with these people through his father, even though he had never been included in any rites or ceremonies. It was not until his father's death that Kabir had developed an interest in the religion, and then mostly because he missed his father so much. Sanskruti was uneasy about his attendance at prayers, but understood her son's growing interest and the comfort it gave him.

Within ten minutes the prayer had ended, and Omar stood, rerolled the mat and replaced it against the wall. The boys walked back through the arched gate. Omar suggested that they go back to the dock until compelled to return to work. Kabir readily agreed.

"Kabir!" a strong, deep, voice called from behind the two of them.

They swung around to face the heavy breathing Malik. Sweat poured down his neck, disappearing into thick clumps of matted hair protruding from his undershirt.

"Yes," Kabir replied.

"Boy, there is a small crate at the railroad station. I want you to take the pull cart and fetch it. Hurry."

Malik clearly believed Kabir was his to command.

The two boys' eyes met in momentary sadness. So much for fun on the dock. That would have to wait for another time. They trotted on ahead so they could curse Malik out of his hearing. They kept their pace for the three blocks to the rear of the factory.

Kabir found the pull cart just inside the rear door. The trip to the station was short, and he had soon returned. He pulled the heavy cart to the front of the building and then went inside to report his arrival to Malik, who was walking the loom room complaining to each woman about her work as he passed. He told Kabir to get Omar to help him unload the crate at the back door.

Kabir walked toward the office where he thought he might find Omar. On the way he saw his mother working at her station and thought he should see if she needed any assistance. He walked to her loom and plopped down beside her, causing her to jump and gasp.

He hadn't intended to startle her, so he moved close to comfort her. He was surprised and saddened to see that her eyes were swollen and red. His first thought was that she had been hurt, and he became immediately defensive.

"What is the matter?" he asked. "Has someone hurt you?"

His mother had seemed on edge for several weeks. She recovered her composure quickly.

"No, you startled me is all," she said, and she turned her face away and went back to her work.

Kabir was not satisfied with her response and asked again, "What is wrong, Mother? You look as though you've been crying."

"Don't worry. I am well," she replied.

She managed a faint smile in his direction. It was another signal, which he understood well. He was not to press her further about the reasons for her tears. He had seen her cry often, especially during the past year since his father's death. He understood that her life had been difficult, although he knew only the sparest reasons for it. There were many mysteries surrounding his mother's life, and he was expected to just accept circumstances without question. In this case, he would never know what cruelty had been spoken or what indignity she had suffered during his absence. He put his hand gently on her shoulder as he explained that he would be gone for a short while to unload the cart in the back. He hesitated as if to add something, but then left without saying it.

CHAPTER TWO

After school the next day, Kabir made for the sari factory at a rapid trot. He was running late because he had lingered too long trading marbles with classmates. He was pleased with his acquisitions—colorful and well formed. He maneuvered through the familiar alleyways, called gallis, of his village, dodging motorbikes, cows, dogs, and goats, while carefully avoiding the filth that littered the timeworn, cobblestone surface. Each block boasted many cramped shops that faced each other across the narrow passage. Most had their doors and windows open in hope the air would dispatch the foul odors of animal waste and garbage. Neither worked, but it was how it had been done for generations. There were people everywhere establishing a constant, relentless clatter that helped define life in the galli. No one really expected it to be different.

While running, Kabir slipped on the patched-stone pavement and took a hard fall in front of the infamous carpenter's shop. He was an elderly man whose bones protruded through his tough, wrinkled skin. He never spoke, but clearly observed everything that went on along his galli. His hands were crooked from years of working with wood, and his teeth had rotted from a life of chewing betel leaves. Rumor had it he had once been a violin virtuoso but couldn't afford to commit his life to the art of music. Others said he was a mute. Then again, they were just rumors. He was famous for his reclusive behavior and awkward ways. Most folks remained leery of him and his intentions, as most folks are of those who choose to remain silent. Kabir glanced at the old man, avoiding eye contact, as he brushed himself off and continued on his way. He detected no malice, but then what was a boy his age to know?

He arrived puffing. It felt good. A good run always made him feel alive. All that soon passed as he entered the big room and the return of its noxious fumes and relentless heat. He settled into the mundane routine that had been his lot for years. He worked the beater, battening the weft threads down tightly as his mother skillfully ran the shuttle back and forth. Together they orchestrated the movements of their hands and fingers in perfect unison, deftly weaving the intricate patterns as the shawl took shape. They had become a good team. Over and over, the rhythm of their movements stacked one layer upon another, making rapid progress as the beautiful design began to appear. With the two of them working, Sanskruti could accomplish a third more than by herself. They kept up their well-practiced, synchronized pace for thirty minutes; an hour; an hour and a half.

As the hours passed, Sanskruti's spirits seemed to lift, putting healing time between her and yesterday's still unspoken incident that had left her wounded. Kabir always had a positive effect on her. He was pleased to see her in a happier mood. Often times they talked as they worked, but that day they both sat silent, each anticipating the movements of the other.

As they neared the end of their work on the final border, Sanskruti softly uttered the ancient words of the weaver's blessing upon the shawl, that good karma would bless the one who wore this work from her heart and hands. As the afternoon wore on, Malik walked down the aisle, dismissing the Muslim weavers for the evening prayer. Kabir usually waited until Malik had passed by them and was outside on his way to the mosque before leaving his mother to join Omar for evening prayer. As he waited for the appropriate moment, Sanskruti put her hand on his arm, causing him to turn back to see what she wanted.

"Kabir," she said softly, looking into his eyes, "Please

don’t leave me. I would like for you to stay with me.”

Most days he would have protested and moaned at such a request, citing the unfairness of it all, but he sensed his mother’s sullenness and nodded his agreement, offering her a smile and a pat on her shoulder. Without a further word, she continued passing the shuttle through the loom and he reached in with the beater and compacted the rows. The work went smoothly. The hours passed into evening. One by one, the workers left their stations and walked out into the night toward their homes.

When Sanskruti and Kabir were at last the only ones left, she laid the shuttle aside and said, “I had hoped to finish this one before we left today, but it is late. Let us go home.”

Kabir was happy to hear that. He had hoped they would leave even sooner but knew that no good would come from suggesting it. His mother was not one to end her workday before a nearly completed shawl was finished. Since this one was more intricate than most, it was taking longer. He figured she had finally succumbed to fatigue. They gathered up their few belongings and waved goodnight to the maintenance man as they left.

Kabir led the way into the warm night with his mother close behind as she arranged her shawl and closed her bag. He inhaled the wonderfully clean, crisp night air as he lingered a moment for her to catch up. They set a quick pace for home. It was a half-hour walk and was already late.

It had always been this way; it was how life was for them. Kabir seldom thought twice about either the long hours in the factory or the long walk home. Their one-room hut was quite modest and served as little more than a place to sleep and keep their bedrolls and a few belongings. Since Sanskruti was an expert sari maker, her income of two hundred rupees a week provided them with a dependable, if modest, amount of food and yarn.

Earlier in the afternoon, his mother had asked Kabir if he had noticed any strangers in the village during the past several days. He said that he hadn't, but her comment set him wondering if that was in some way connected to her apparent recent anxiety.

The sky above darkened. The shadow-laden passageways between buildings assumed the blackened nighttime mantle first. A few all-night factories remained lit in the distance. Sanskruti suddenly regretted that she had remained so late at her work. What little protection and dignity she had known disappeared with the death of her husband, Shahid, just a year before. It was a grueling life they had chosen when they fell in love. Neither his Muslim family nor her Hindu family would support their marriage, so baby Kabir had been born out of wedlock. There were few things that a young couple could do to ensure against their being forever ostracized. Yet their love compelled them. Over eleven years, their attempts to redeem themselves in the eyes of both religions had been blocked by generations of tradition and had fallen on deaf ears, even within their families.

Sanskruti felt a cold chill, despite the relative warmth of the night, and drew her thin shawl more tightly around her. The two spoke little, Sanskruti thinking of her lifelong plight and Kabir reluctant to speak of his activities planned with Omar for the next day. As they continued through the darkened village, she was startled by an unfamiliar, misplaced noise from up ahead. She stopped and cocked her head into the darkness, hoping to make sense of it.

"Why do you stop, Ma?" Kabir asked. "Is something wrong?"

He, too, leaned his head into the darkness ahead but could make out nothing unusual. He studied his mother for a moment as she stared into the night, a look of fear plainly growing on her face. He moved closer to her, taking on her fear but not understanding why.

Then, he also heard it. Unfamiliar. Out of place. Perhaps a man's heavy breathing punctuated with a rolling, guttural wheeze. Perhaps bold, private whispers between men. It was not unusual to hear or meet people in these streets on their way home at night, but in fact, the streets were uncommonly empty. His mother's sudden cautious attentiveness grew the fright within him. He stared ahead where the path was no longer lit, and strained to see what might be waiting in the shadows. He could see nothing.

Sanskruti whispered to him, "Follow me."

She turned slowly and started back the way they had come. Kabir was perplexed, but followed.

“Why? What is the matter? You’re going the wrong way!”

She did not reply, but quickened her pace back toward the lighted shops, searching them with a degree of desperation to see if any might still have a merchant inside. Kabir followed, alternately watching his mother and glancing back over his shoulder to see if he could determine what had spooked her.

“Is there something? Why do we walk this way now? Tell me!”

Still, she said nothing, scanning the shops for any sign of life. That low, droning noise still behind them became louder and closer. Kabir glanced backward, thinking he saw movement in the shadows beyond the light. He may have also heard heavy, irregular footsteps picking up speed faster and faster.

“There is something back there, Mother. I saw it.”

Sanskruti again picked up her pace. Fear and anxiety showed on her face. Her eyes darted one way and the other in search of refuge or help. Kabir had never witnessed such terror in her.

“Mother. What is it? Why are you frightened? Who is that?” he asked, leaving all pretense of the whisper behind.

He was bothered and increasingly alarmed by her unwillingness to explain. Danger felt imminent.

Sanskruti hurried on. They were virtually running down the street. Kabir's legs grew weak, and his heart pounded as fear morphed into panic .

They approached an alleyway off to their right and, with a tug to his sleeve, Sanskruti guided Kabir into the gallis's unexplored darkness. It seemed their best, their only, option.

They fled west down the gallis, desperate to disappear into the plentiful shadows. There was no total cloak of darkness that night. The moon was full and betrayed their position. It became clear that the shadows offered only faint refuge. It was long after evening prayer, so there was little chance anyone would hear or see them and come to their aid. Even if they would try to force the issue with screams, it was almost certain that prejudice forbade their rescue.

"Toward the river," she directed, panting, nearly out of breath, as much from fear as from the weariness caused by their exhausting retreat.

Kabir had spotted the silhouetted figure pursuing them from the main street but dared not look again for fear of tripping or losing contact with his mother. These were the most terrifying moments of his life.

They made their way along the bank, crouching behind anything that would hide or disguise them and their shadows. Was it better to creep with stealth, hoping not to be seen, or safer to run and hope to outdistance the pursuer? They tried to move quietly, but in the silence of the evening, their footsteps could be heard even in the dry powdered dust that covered the ground. Kabir noted to himself that even his breathing seemed too loud as they wove a path along the river. They stopped behind a stand of thornbushes and cautiously looked back. Their pursuer no longer attempted to stay hidden. Definitely a man. Kabir had never seen him before. He was bald with a long, dark beard. He stopped some sixty feet away. He was not breathing hard, which made Kabir think he might be an athlete.

Oddly, the man began humming an eerie song, as he looked one way and then another. It was one Kabir had never heard. Something about it was fully unnerving. It might well have been a dirge. He figured that perhaps the man was from some distant place with different songs. The humming continued as his search became methodical.

Fear paralyzed Kabir. He continued to wonder why this man was chasing them. What have we done? he asked himself. He must know we have nothing of value. We are like baby birds, out here in an open nest trying to hide from a condor. Can he see us? Can he catch us? What will he do to us?

"Do you know the tune?" he asked in a whisper.

"Yes. Hurry, now!"

She tugged on him again. They remained bent over and moved on through the cover of the thorny underbrush. They came upon the upper steps of a ghat. Thinking they might make an escape in one of the boats or at least be able to hide among them, Sanskruti pushed Kabir on ahead of her, pointing. They raced down the steep steps and were by then out in the open. The man spotted them. At the water's edge, dozens of small wooden boats were lined up, tied to iron rings set into the lowest step.

There would not be time to untie one and get away. The best Sanskruti could hope for was to find a place to hide, hoping death would pass them by. The boats swayed, knocking against those on each side, setting up a quiet, rhythmic pattern as if drums in the forest. Between the moon's great size and its reflection off the water, it seemed to illuminate every crevice. As a cloud momentarily blocked the moon, mother and son ducked behind a stack of pallets and paused while Sanskruti decided how to proceed. They heard hatred's footsteps coming ever closer.

Sanskruti understood what was taking place. It had been her fear for years. Again she pointed, and two of them slipped into the water and waded toward the rear of the line of boats.

"Keep low, close to the boats," she directed.

The water was deep and Sanskruti supported Kabir, whose feet could not touch bottom. They stopped at the rear of a large boat. It was as far as she could go. Sanskruti pulled her son's head close, holding his face against her lips.

"If I let you go, you must swim downstream and hide

there," she instructed. "The flow of the water will assist you. Make your way swiftly and quietly."

Kabir understood her words but not their meaning.

As the boy's young limbs wrapped ever more tightly around her neck and torso, Sanskruti felt her bare feet sinking ankle deep into the mud below.

Sanskruti heard the man as he began sloshing through the water, searching between and behind every boat in the line. He was so close she could hear his heavy breathing. At that point, she kissed Kabir on his forehead and gently pried free of his embrace. She turned him toward the open water and commended him to the protection of the sacred river.

"I love you, Son. Now swim! Swim as far as you can and hide. I will follow."

She knew she would not follow. Her feet were held fast by the mire. She could not move. Instead, she began beating on the rear of the boat, hoping to attract the man's attention so her beloved son could slip beyond his sight.

Kabir's slim, dark body glided far out into the river and became swept up in the current before he took his first, meaningful stroke. With virtually no effort on his part, the swift current carried him downstream. He turned once, looking for his mother. He saw nothing but the moon's reflection on that never-ending expanse of water.

Looking again downstream, all he could see was the light from the moon dancing along the low crests of the ripples as they played along the bank and brushed along the boats and ghat. He was unaware of how fast the silent current was moving him. Pockets of cold water rose from below and swirled around his torso as if trying to engage him in a game of tickle.

As he realized he was being carried away, he began to feel the downward tug of the current from below. He struggled to keep afloat, but his head was soon sucked below the surface. He kicked hard and pulled at the water with all his strength, attempting to raise his head through the surface and grab a breath of air. At that moment, any air would do, even the foul air from inside the factory. Just as his strength vanished and he surrendered to the current, his head popped above the surface. His struggle had saved him.

At first he had no idea which direction he was facing. He turned to move with the water, struggling to engage his arms and legs again, but his exhausted limbs were useless. He rolled over onto his back and was able to keep his face up and his body afloat. His instinct, however, was to confront the river on his stomach, which caused him to sink over and over again. Gasping and fighting to keep his head above the water, and being quite sure he had by then escaped the man, he managed to scream, but his cries were drowned by the water rushing into his open mouth. Clouds had covered the moon again, so the world above the water was black and foreboding. The noise of the rushing water muffled any sounds from shore. He felt totally alone for the first time in his life.

Exhausted and coughing up water, he lay motionless on his back in the mud of the bank. He heard male voices, confusion, angst. He wondered if the man giving chase had finally caught up. Despite his fear, he was too fatigued to swim away. He just lay there, eyes closed, his senses overwhelmed, his heart pounding, feeling a discomforting swirl of relief, anger, and terror deep within.

Eventually Kabir was able to look up. He was gazing into a face, blurred by his burning eyes. The man staring down at him was neither bald nor bearded. Others were staring at him too. He felt safe.

“Where is my mother”? Kabir managed aloud at last.

The stranger remained silent.

Kabir trembled, wondering whether his mother had escaped too, and whether, as promised, she was behind him, trying to catch up. What had happened to her? Where did the river bring me? How can I find her? How will she find me?

Questions raced through his mind and tears went unnoticed against his already wet face.

The pounding in his ears that had made him virtually deaf to human voices began to dissipate. His heart began to quiet, as did the throbbing and noise inside his head.

He heard someone say, “I wonder if his mother who he’s been mumbling about is dead.”

Then another, "She brought this upon herself and her son, you know. We best have no part in it."

These words sank like wedges driven deeply into Kabir. They did, however, indicate the men knew of him. He heard them leave.

Kabir tried to lift his head. He couldn't. He struggled to call out but nothing would escape his swollen tongue. The strong arms of a man who had been standing over him reached down and cradled Kabir. In the darkness, Kabir still could not make out the man's face. The stranger smelled like newly laid sawdust on the floor in a horse stable.

The man draped a shawl over Kabir's wet, shivering body. He carried the boy to an office in a nearby factory. It was warm as if there were a stove there. The man removed Kabir's soaked long shirt, dried him as best he could, and wrapped his naked body in a dry, woolen shawl. He leaned him against a wall and brought him a tiny cup of hot tea. Kabir sat grasping the cup, which brought welcome warmth to his cold bony fingers and pruned palms. All he could manage was to sit and stare into his tea. Just holding the warm porcelain cup was tiring. Kabir found himself drifting off to sleep amid questions about his mother. He swirled in and out of consciousness.

CHAPTER THREE

Kabir had a fitful sleep. Shortly after dawn, he was awakened by the usual early morning sounds of revving engines and honking horns. He found himself alone back inside his own hut, confused by how he got there. The events of the night remained a blur—a blur accompanied by an unexplained sense of intense terror. It set his stomach churning and his heart racing.

There on the stool, which he often used for a table, he found bread. Wiping his eyes, he sat listening to the sounds outside. They seemed louder and more obnoxious than usual. He tried to block them out, munching on the bread, thankful he was alive. The air was damp and cold. He would surely find a drizzly day outside.

He looked around, expecting to see his mother, but she wasn't there. He was suddenly deluged with sights and memories of the prior night's flight and the large, bald, amply whiskered man chasing them, the escape into the river, his mother releasing him into the current, and her final embrace. His heart began to race again as he relived the awful events and remembered his final vision of her wonderful face.

The sounds of the morning were broken by the call for prayer. "Alla-a-a-ahu Akbar ...," the Islamic words were well known to him as they had pierced the air five times a day for his entire life. He mouthed them as he ate. "God is the greatest. I bear witness that there is no deity except Allah."

As he sat alone, munching and pondering the events of the previous night, he heard the faint sound of raindrops on the tin roof above. He looked outside. The cloud-dimmed morning light left the hut dark. The floor—laden with shadows—and the walls grew colorless. Profound grief grew inside him as he wondered about his mother's fate. As these feelings swelled, tears again left trails down his stoic face. He turned from the window back to the stool and as if from out of the humid morning air itself, he found a fresh cup of warm tea sitting there. Without questions, he took it and began to sip. The mild aroma of chai soothed his anxious spirit. What do I do now? he wondered. He had to find his mother. Would she return? Would he ever see her again?

The tea was soon gone but the cup remained warm. He held it between his palms for a long moment, contemplating both its warmth and its emptiness. Eventually, he placed it on the floor beside the door. He raised his arms for the first time, pulling the shawl up over his head. Covering his head would help keep him warm and hide the now uncontrollable tears streaming down his face. Kabir wasn't sure he wanted them to stop. He pulled his feet inside the shawl and leaned against the loom. Soon exhaustion again overcame him. He lay down and drifted off to sleep.

He heard the thunderclap and rain bounce loudly upon the roof, sensing the bright flashes of lightning through his closed eyes. Even in sleep, the fright would not leave.

Then, there it was, the always calming sound of his mother's voice singing his favorite lullaby. Awake it could not be. Asleep it was his ultimate comfort, his one true source of unfailing security. In his dream world, she could always be right there at his side.

As she sang, he felt her fingers stroking his face. Each time he gazed upon her gentle smile, she raised her hand, fingers spread, each one reflecting a river of India. It was their game. Then they were walking. He held his mother's hand and carried leeks for soup. He hung back to kick some pebbles. It didn't work so well so he ran a bit to catch up. Arriving at home, she started a fire and hung their small pot above the flame. As the water boiled, his mother lay in cut leeks and dropped in spices from her hand. It smelled intoxicating as they squatted around the boiling pot anticipating the evening meal.

As he stretched himself back into wakefulness, that nighttime paradise slowly faded, replaced by memories of the real world, his brand new, all alone, very scary, real world.

Again, worry whirled inside his head. He had no time for self-pity. He needed a plan to cheat death

Kabir struggled into his long shirt that had dried even through the humidity of the day. The impulse to run outside and look for his mother carried him out the front door and onto the unpaved path. It was muddy after the rain and provided poor traction for his bare feet. He ran up the main street, heading toward the place where he last saw her. He quickly became winded, still weak from his ordeal in the river. He paused, bent over, hands on his knees to catch his breath. Then, he ran for several hundred more yards before slowing to a walk. He reached the site of the white painted grocer's stand with its wares stacked out front against its mud-splattered walls. There was still some foot traffic in the street. Kabir trailed behind several familiar people as they meandered past the junkyards toward the river. It was the best source of safety he could manage.

As he came upon the top of the nearest ghat, just short of the stand of thornbushes, he quickened his pace and his heart began beating frantically. At the bottom of the steps, near the edge of the river, he saw a group of villagers. They were speaking in low tones. He slowed as he descended the final few steps. When he approached them, they looked up, sadness, perhaps even compassion, was clear upon the faces of those who recognized him. Kabir stopped and stood in silence, afraid to ask the obvious. He studied their faces for clues. Most of them lowered their eyes, no one wanting to bear the sad tidings.

"Ma!" he cried, both asking about her fate and confessing that he knew. Two of the women left the scene, passing close to Kabir. One paused to touch his shoulder.

He looked up at her old face.

"Is she dead?" he asked though his tears.

The woman nodded. Her lower lip trembled, and she moved on up the steps.

Kabir ran to a grassy area just back from the top of the ghat. He sank to the ground, sitting on the damp earth, his legs beneath him. He wept. The remaining onlookers soon finished their conversations and left the scene in twos and threes. None offered so much as a word of condolence or even acknowledged his presence. Before long, the boy sat alone with his sobbing, his heaving chest, and tear-dampened cheeks and shirt.

He remained alone with his grief and stared into a nearby acacia thicket. With his eyes he retraced their frantic dash down the steps to the water's edge. She was well then, without injury except for some thorn punctures. Who knew what had happened to her. Probably the bald man knew. Kabir didn't want to know the details. It was clear that her life was over. He would never bask in her smile again; her voice would no longer sing to comfort him; her long gentle fingers would never rub his back to bring sleep at night. He looked around, wondering where they had taken her body. It didn't really matter, he thought. There was nothing he could do for her in death.

Kabir stood and looked up into the darkening evening sky. He descended the steps once more and began walking alongside the Ganges until he came upon one of the ghats where funeral pyres lined the bank, waiting to be lit in the darkness of the night. He moved on to the Manikarnika ghat and made his way across the wide stone steps along the lower bank of the river. With the dark sky and the silver water as a backdrop, raging pyres burned brightly along the holy Ganges. Suffocating smoke and ash rendered the hot air heavy and unpleasant. He began sweating from the heat of the flames. A bit further on, he found a place to sit on the edge of a pyre not yet lit.

A body wrapped in white cloth, adorned with garlands of yellow flowers, waited atop logs and twigs. It seemed peaceful there, away from the crowd and other bodies awaiting cremation.

"Hey, kid, come here. Help me," a wrinkled old man signaled Kabir.

Kabir didn't acknowledge the old man. He didn't want anyone's company.

The old man continued.

"Help me. There are jewels and gold teeth down there in the water. Let's find it".

He pointed to two corpses covered in ash as they floated away from the bank.

Kabir was still not moved to be of assistance.

"Useless kid!"

The old man spat paan juice into the river and moved on down the line.

Another man arrived with a torch. Kabir rose and stepped back. As the torch was laid upon the pyre, Kabir pretended it was his mother. He watched as it was consumed. There was a beauty about it, he thought. He listened to the rhythmic crackling and watched sparks rise, dim, and go out. It was the only way he had of giving his mother a funeral. He felt better, still sad but somehow better. He noticed that his tears had stopped. The nature of the fright within him had been unlocked from the night before and had been assumed by his fright about his immediate future.

CHAPTER FOUR

Two weeks had passed since Kabir spent his first night alone in what had been *their* humble hut. It shared outer walls with the huts of other families. The area, his village, comprised a labyrinth of hovels borrowing support from the common walls. The hovel walls were built with flat stones and broken pieces of concrete salvaged from dilapidated structures. They were stacked just five feet. Only recently had Kabir begun to notice the need to slouch as he entered through the low opening. The stones were mortared together with mud that he and his mother had carried from the banks of the river. It was mixed with a confetti of dry leaves and pine needles that made a surprisingly strong adhesive. From time to time the mud mixture had to be repaired or replaced. His hut had a metal roof, a great luxury compared with those that were merely thatched.

As new living spaces were needed, the area expanded, wall against wall. There was no plan. It just grew south and west into available space. Down through the centuries it had become like an ever-expanding collective honeycomb growing to accommodate a seemingly endless supply of new people. It was limited only by the availability of necessary materials. Narrow corridors meandered between rows of dwellings. Many of them were barely large enough for an adult to pass through.

Kabir's eyes drifted to the ceiling of his poorly lit hut. The original roof had been made from reclaimed timber from collapsed buildings and dried branches from fallen trees. Dried palm stalks and layers of dried thatch were interwoven and tightly stretched across the primary supports. This allowed precipitation to run off the roofs onto the paths between the hovels, which, during storms, also served as drainage ditches. Most residents there were forced to gather replacement material to make repairs after torrents of rain destroyed parts of their roof. His father had scavenged metal sheeting, which he placed over the thatch. They always remained dry inside and considerably cooler in summer and warmer in winter than their neighbors.

They harvested clay from beneath the barren topsoil, wetting it into a thick paste to spread as a type of stucco to cover the floors inside their dwellings. It dried hard and tough. As layers of clay had been added to his hut over the years, the height of the floor had been raised to prevent rain and sewage from running inside. Kabir was ever vigilant to watch for extra dried reeds, vegetation, and wood to give their neighbors for repairs or to use as kindling in their own fires. They all were careful to observe gracious customs of privacy and good manners, often difficult when living elbow to elbow.

Kabir had stayed to himself since that dreadful night by the river. He stopped going to school and had not returned to the factory. Morsels of bread and a few vegetables were often left in his hut while he slept or was away. He would find them sitting on his stool. His benefactor was unknown. Such gifts came three, sometimes four times a week. Even though those meals were scanty and plain, they were far better than the nights he had to go to sleep without anything. He was often awakened in the predawn hours by gnawing pangs of hunger. He had occasionally gone to the local canteen to beg with other children for trimmings from the tables. Again, he was grateful. He often thought about the things that brought him pleasure. Since his mother's death, that was almost always food.

One morning, several weeks later, he awoke to a different set of feelings, less sad and less helpless. Kabir finally acknowledged that he would have to fend for himself and decided to go to back to the factory and see if a full-time position was available. He took his bread with him as he left the hut and walked down the dusty dirt road toward the village. He had forgotten how long a walk it was. Perhaps it just seemed that way because he didn't have his mother to talk with.

He entered the familiar, rambling old building. Oddly, he thought, it seemed comforting. Kabir had virtually been raised inside its poorly lit rooms. He had learned to weave and work the loom from his mother. As he made his way back through the looms, he noticed that everyone was staring at him. He continued on to his mother's loom and sat on the sofreh. The shuttle was still sitting at the far left of the harness. Her unfinished shawl was still set up in the loom. It was a pattern his mother had worked many times. He knew it well. It was the traditional Hindu flora motif of the pinecone woven into patterns for brocade. Without approaching Malik first, he picked up the shuttle and set it in motion, weaving the weft threads back and forth then battening them down tight with the reed comb. For three hours he sat weaving the elaborate pattern. It felt good. It felt like home. As he gained familiarity with the process, he picked up speed.

Malik, who had been away, entered the room and walked through, making his rounds. In his gruff way he reminded each of the weavers about their deadlines. He stopped and stood above Kabir. He bent in close and examined the boy's work. He nodded—almost smiled—obviously surprised at its quality.

"Your mother may be gone, but you may take her place. Since you are only a boy I will pay you two rupees for every sari." Kabir said nothing, nor did he need to. He had just taken his mother's place, if for only half the meager amount she had received.

As Kabir sat weaving, his nimble fingers worked quickly, requiring little deliberation. He thought about the only family he had known and fantasized about being reunited with his grandfather one day. His mother's father was the only living family about which he had ever heard his mother speak, and she had not made it clear why they never saw him. He lived in some far off city, to the north he thought. Kabir tried to imagine the details of the goatee on his grandfather's face, the shape of his smile and tone of his voice, all as his mother had described them. Maybe his grandfather would find and kill the man who had taken his mother's life. At that time, more than ever, he longed for the protection he lost when his father died. Now, he had none at all.

Weaving next to his mother there at the factory, he had never felt alone or unsafe. She answered and explained many of Kabir's questions, and they talked freely about a wide variety of things. Occasionally, she would even discuss remembrances of his father and life before he was born. Now, with his mother no longer beside him, Kabir relived those conversations within himself.

From time to time, Kabir overheard his mother's name mentioned in whispers behind him. He listened intently while feigning his attention on the loom.

"Was anyone questioned by the police about Sanskruti's killing?" asked one of the women in low tones.

"I don't know, but my husband says many of the men in the village are fearful that her death will bring unfavorable attention to the area," replied the wife of Sheikh Abdul.

It seemed his mother was being blamed for the consequences of her own death.

That conversation was interrupted by the call to prayer, "Alla-a-a-ahu Akbar ..."

Malik quickly walked through the factory carrying his valuable prayer mat and released those who were ready to end their labors for the day. He then approached Kabir.

"This sari has to be finished today."

Kabir had heard that tone of voice before.

"You know what happens if you can't get your work done."

Malik had never made a secret of his dislike for the boy—Hindu, child of a mixed religious background, and a bastard on top of it all. For years he had held in his rage about the waif. Perhaps it was his mother's presence that had protected him. Kabir had witnessed Malik's rage before, but had seldom been on the receiving end of it. Mr. Malik went into his office and returned with a whip. His irrational anger grew, well out of proportion to the topic, Kabir thought. He had every intention of finishing the sari. There had been no back-talk or any indication of disrespect.

Malik's face reddened. The situation grew frightening and he wanted to run. Malik raised the whip. The boy clinched his fist, preparing to fight back, but with the first sting laid onto his back his energy drained away. He slumped to his knees as strike after strike continued. The pain became unbearable. The blood from the openings on his back drenched his shirt. Kabir fell in and out of consciousness. He forced himself to think about swimming in the Ganges and feeling the cool water on his body. He tried to think about the warmth of his mother's embrace and the smell of jasmine on her silk sari. None of that helped.

In the end, Kabir lay there in the corner, disoriented and wishing it had been he and not his mother who had died.

With great effort, he eventually returned to the loom and finished the little bit that remained. When he finally found the strength to leave the factory, the sun was below the horizon and reflected a brilliant pink tint across the clouds in the west. He gathered sticks and twigs along the way to build a fire that night to heat his meal, but the pain from the whipping led him to want to just curl up motionless on his sleeping mat.

The weather was becoming cooler and he could see that

the short summer was beginning to fade. He knew it was time to begin laying in larger pieces of wood to keep his tiny hut warm through the nights and to have a supply of fuel for cooking. All of that was now his responsibility. It highlighted the fact that he was indeed on his own.

Slowly, he made his way along the dusty road and eventually entered the last row of shops before coming to his hut. The street and shops seemed busy as usual, with people bartering for goods and stopping for a drink of coffee before heading home for the night.

He noticed a man leaning against the wall of the supply store, smoking. He was dressed in long black pants that were expensive looking and covered in dust. He also wore a collared, gray plaid shirt with short sleeves, and he brandished a gold watch on his left wrist. His hair was gray and curly; his eyebrows bushy and thick, with a chin beard to match.

It was, however, the man's piercing glare that telegraphed an uneasy darkness about him. His eyes remained half-closed as if he were studying Kabir. It caused the boy to turn away, hoping to avoid further notice. A clandestine glance a few moments later found the man still staring into the street, perhaps focused on him. Kabir moved to gather twigs under an old tree on the far side of the street, avoiding the need for any direct encounter. He then hurried along the dirt path, adding to his supply of firewood as he went. The sudden appearance of sinister-looking men in his life was unnerving. Old terrors returned.

When Kabir entered his hut, he dropped the pile of twigs onto the floor and arranged some of them inside his stone cooking area. He soon had a low fire going, set with sparks from his flint and stone. He boiled a small pot of water, cut up his vegetables, and dropped them into the simmering pot. He poured himself a drink of water and put the rest into the largest pan he had. He removed his blood-stained shirt and repeatedly dipped it in and out, hoping to remove as much of the stain as possible. He had learned cold water worked best on blood and the sooner treated, the more completely it worked.

As he prepared his meal, he could hear the nearby families in their huts and quietly kept company with his unsuspecting neighbors. He was exhausted following his interminable and hurt-filled day at the factory. He let the beating go. It came with who he was. He forgot about the man with the piercing gaze. He ate, banked the fire for the night, and was soon asleep.

CHAPTER FIVE

The next morning, Kabir returned to the factory. He continued toiling there day after day. It came to him that he had spent nearly every waking moment of his life there. The weeks passed, and he listened to the conversations that whirled and churned in the disgusting factory air. The seasons changed. Summer came upon them. Days blurred into months until the following summer had come and gone. Another season came, and then another and another. Seasons meant little to him. The factory was always uncomfortable, too hot in the summer and too cold in the winter.

Three years had passed since the death of his mother. Kabir turned thirteen. As he sat working at her loom most hours of every day, the comforting memories of her kind smile and loving voice were with him. He continued doing her work, still for half her pay.

The stability of Kabir's life began to erode. At the factory, Kabir was no longer required to weave the finer, more intricate time-consuming designs that women seemed to handle more easily. He and Omar spent more and more of their time running shipments to urban and rural customers. Omar's father would make trucks available to them. Even their visits to the mosque had dwindled to just morning prayer. They missed the reassurance of the ritual. They missed the tradition.

Kabir's daily activities were no longer filled with satisfaction or pride. His mind lacked focus and his nights were lonely and sleepless. Even the conversations of his neighbors, which pierced the walls of his hut, no longer amused him or drove away his loneliness. They became a nuisance, as husbands and wives seemed to argue with far greater frequency. More anger was evident than before. He could feel himself being swept away down a river of irrelevant consequence. He felt as suffocated and tired as he had those many years before while fighting his way through the darkened, churning waters of the River Ganges.

It was Saturday, bathing day at the river. Kabir was excited because this was his favorite routine of the week. It had changed very little from childhood. Once a week he would gather with his neighbors on the bank of the river. Leaving their cloths behind, they waded gleefully into the river to wash and splash. It was a place where the cheerful squeals of frolicking children were dependably present. Kabir liked to wade far out into the river where the water was cleaner and where less debris floated past. The water flowed faster out there and he liked it, as it seemed to engage him, tugging and pushing at his skin.

The Ganges is the lifeline of India. Flowing from the majestic Himalayas through the Bengal, Kabir felt privileged to live near the vicinity of its path. In Varanasi, the Ganges flows quietly past the various ghats, its dark waters alluring and mythical. Children giggle as they swim, mourners cry while dead bodies of loved ones are swept away, fisherman are grateful for the fish, and worshipers are in awe of the divine presence.

Bathing day was less a chore or ritual of hygiene than it was an occasion of shared joy and thanks. Mothers joyfully dipped their little ones in and out of the river. It was a time for families to caress and acknowledge one another's worth. For those few minutes each week, cares were left on the bank. And all of his neighbors had cares. Even though he had no one of his own, the joy and thanksgiving remained and felt satisfying to him.

Kabir longed for the intense heat of the summer, which, by comparison, made the unvarying water temperature seem cooler and more refreshing. The best part of summer was allowing the warmth of the sun and the dry winds to blow across his skin, drying his body in minutes. Bathing day was also when he washed his dingy, tattered long shirt in the river, carrying it back to his hut draped over his shoulder. He would fling it out flat over the hot metal of his roof to dry.

That morning, Kabir finished bathing even before the sun had fully risen. His shirt dried quickly in the morning breeze. Few things got underway before the blazing morning sun had dispatched the darkness. That day, he visited the small collection of shops near his home. The grocer stand was not yet open, its heavy wooden shutters still covered the openings along the face of its weathered walls. The laundry always opened early. As he passed by he could hear the women inside, chatting and sloshing tubs of clothes with their large wooden paddles.

In the distance, he could hear swarms of swallows awakening to the sun's light and the thunderous flapping of their wings as they flew together to the river for their morning drink and bath. The large trees in the distance teamed with hundreds—more likely, thousands—of the noisy birds. As he walked farther down the path, the shops ended and the roadsides became crowded with thick undergrowth. There was an occasional building set back from the road. They were often surrounded by rock walls and protected by large rusting-iron gates, most of which remained closed at that hour.

During the months that passed, Kabir had engaged in lots of serious thinking about his life, and for the first time really began asking himself what he wanted to do with it. Certainly there could be more than working long hours at the factory and enduring the abuse from Malik. Perhaps he could work in a shop, but most of them were family run. Perhaps a life on the river would suit him.

He made his way back to the water and walked the bank.

The River Ganges plays a central, religious role in the lives of Hindus, as well as holds an important place in the country's commerce. To bathe in its waters, especially at the bathing ghats of Varanasi—at least once during a lifetime—is considered essential in ones quest for nirvana. It is a long river stretching nearly the width and length of India. It springs from a trickle in the Himalayas. At Varanasi it is very wide and most days renders a relatively smooth surface that tires the eyes as it reflects the relentlessly hot sun.

This day, the banks of the river were lined with the ghats leading into the river. Kabir had heard there were more than one hundred of these small stairways along the banks at Varanasi. Many were bathing ghats, like the one Kabir had visited earlier that morning. Some were cremation ghats. His most vivid memory of these was laced in sadness. Large, many-storied brick-and-stone buildings served as backdrops. Some were so tall they seemed to descend from the heavens themselves. The legion of steps that defined the ghats flowed like waterfalls from the front doors of those stately old edifices into the water of the great river.

Kabir moved on north to the boat ghats. Boats would come into dock and they would leave for destinations about which the boy could only wonder. They were loaded and unloaded. Some were large. Others were small vessels. Some carried cargo. Some transported people. Still others took tourists on sightseeing trips, up the river and then back. Many of these people came from faraway places, and Kabir figured they would have wonderful stories to relate about areas of the world he had never even dreamed about. He loved to hear and later retell such stories sometimes, changing them a bit to fit his creative fantasies.

In some places the small tourist boats were moored so tightly together that you could easily step from one to another and make your way for an extended distance. They were mostly open boats propelled by strong men with bamboo paddles. A few had motors on the back. A few of these had shade screens stretched high between four vertical poles. He assumed it cost tourists more to ride in them. Many were unpainted or at the most had a single wide line of color painted along the upper edge. Most looked capable of carrying from eight to twelve passengers.

Perhaps a quarter of them had the traditional seats familiar to most rowboats, those that crossed the boat from side to side each seating two to three passengers. There would be little opportunity to mix with the tourists in such boats and hear their stories, since the boatmen, called boatwalas, sat in the rear. Most, however, had the seating arranged around the perimeter so guests sat facing each other across the boat. In these, he noticed, the guests often stood, mingling in the open area. That probably provided a better view, he imagined. The bottoms in these appeared to be flat. Perhaps there was a floor added above the curved bottom of the craft for the comfort of those who rode in them. At any rate, they appeared to be far more expensive than the smaller ones with traditional seats.

The larger and sturdier boats seemed to have more favorable docking privileges. He figured as tourist boats went, they provided the longer and more expensive tours to passengers who were probably seasoned travelers and, therefore, more interesting to speak with. He wondered how one became a boatwala. He studied the possibilities as he made his way down the wide, crumbling stone steps of the ghat toward where one particularly substantial, impressive boat was tied up. Even the handles of the paddles were painted.

He approached the boatwala who seemed to be in charge there.

"How do I get a job on your boat?"

It was a straightforward, if naïve, question.

"How long you been a boatwala?"

"I'm not, but I think I might want to be."

The man chuckled into his hand.

"Well, son, come back and see me after you've been on the water six months. You look a bit young but seem strong for your size and you are handsome. Boats like this need strong, good-looking men to attract the best tourists. Get some experience and then come back and see me."

Kabir had learned an important lesson—experience on the river counted for everything, and his time at the factory counted for nothing. He didn't let that encounter deter him. He moved on to the area of the medium-size boats and repeated his question to several of the men. He received similar answers—brush-offs were more like it. One took time to examine the palms of his hands then shook his head. It had been another useful lesson.

Kabir studied the hands of the nearby boatwalas and he understood. He had no calluses. It seemed to be a prerequisite. His years at the loom in the sari factory had neither required nor produced hardened palms. If I could only row with my feet, he thought. He smiled to himself. He moved on down the line of boats.

Eventually he came to a small red rowboat at the very end of the line. No one was there, so he got in and sat at the rear, holding a paddle in his hands. He dipped it into the river and pulled it back toward him through the water.

"This feels right," he said out loud.

The words surprised him. He smiled and nodded. He

felt good.

"Hey there. What you doing?" came words from behind him.

He turned in the seat to see a small-boned old man, stripped to the waist, standing there with his hands on his hips.

"This yours?" Kabir asked.

"It is."

"I've been thinking about becoming a boatwala and since this boat was empty I thought I'd try to get a feel for how it would . . . well, feel. I meant no harm."

"None done. Ever paddle?"

"No, sir. Never. Well, just now. Once."

His rambling was clearly not helping him make a good impression.

"Get seasick?"

"Don't know. Never been on water in a boat."

To that point he felt he was surely striking out.

"You good with people?"

"I think so. Have some problems with a boss at the sari factory where I work ,and I'm not yet very experienced talking with girls, but adults have mostly seemed to like me. I guess I'm more of a loner. I have one close friend, though."

He knew he was rambling again, so he stopped.

"Stand up."

Somewhat awkwardly, Kabir returned the paddle more

or less to where he remembered it had been stashed. He stood facing forward then turned in careful, tiny steps to face the man. Overturning the boat at that point would certainly not be in his favor. The old man looked the boy over. Out of recent experience Kabir held out his hands, palms up. He was honest if not in any way qualified.

"I'm not yet calloused as you can see, but I'm willing to work at it. I'm a good worker and not afraid of long hours."

"My partner left to take care of family. Won't be back anytime soon. I can use help—strong, young help. You seem to fit the bill. Got family to support?"

"No, sir. Just me. My mother died sometime back."

He wondered if he should have answered "yes," thinking a family to support might have gotten him more money.

"Tell you what. I'll give you two meals a day and a small salary. That'll depend on how well you work out. We'll give it a month. Think of it as gaining good experience. If you do well and like it, I know you'll eventually move on to a better boat. That's okay. I understand how it is to be young and ambitious."

Kabir had never thought of himself as either ambitious or unambitious. For that matter, he had never thought of himself as young. He had always just been who he was at that moment.

"Got a place to live?" the old man asked.

"Yes, sir. The hut I was raised in. It's fine for me."

"Be here at sunup tomorrow. Bring rags to wrap your hands. Got salve?"

"A little."

"Probably need it before the day's over. We work 'til evening prayers."

The man was Hindu. All the boatwalas were. That should be comfortable, and different, working for a Hindu alongside other Hindus. Kabir had heard that it was the privilege of working on the sacred river that encouraged many young Hindu men to enter the vocation. He wondered if he should relate the story of his own mixed religious upbringing. He chose to remain silent on the topic. His experience in that area had generally not been good. If it became necessary, he could discuss the subject later on.

CHAPTER SIX

Kabir was more excited than he thought he would be. Sleep came hard and lasted but a short time. He figured that since he had finished the last sari on which he had been working at the factory, and since he had been paid for that day's work, he didn't owe Malik a formal resignation.

Sometime during the night, bread had arrived. It was more than before. He took some of it with him and left the rest behind for later. He had to wonder if the secret donor knew about his strenuous day ahead. The night before, he had prepared rags from one of his mother's garments. He felt it was right that part of her should be with him that day.

He had lots of wonders that morning as he made his

way through the predawn darkness toward the tourist ghat. Where would they be going? Would they stay busy all day? Would he be expected to paddle all day? How much would he be paid? Kabir understood that good effort would translate into more money; that had been the man's promise. Rumor had it that boatwalas made a very good wage. He wasn't sure what that meant but had heard that tourists paid up to fifty rupees a tour. At four tours a day that came to be more money than he could imagine. His heart raced with anticipation. Perhaps someday he could own his own boat.

It was only his second job. Think of that, he thought to himself. Thirteen years old and I've only ever had one job!

The roads were empty except for the stray goat or cow. The village had not yet awakened. Kabir finished his bread long before he arrived at the Ganges. The day before, he noticed all the boatwalas chewed paan—betel leaves rolled around tobacco. Most men from the village did. Many children did as well. Kabir's mother had forbidden him to use it, citing the unattractive discoloration and deterioration of the teeth it caused. He had tried it, of course—he *was* a boy, after all—but really didn't like it and was seldom pressured into doing things he didn't want to do. Omar had begun several years before, and Kabir rode him about it all the time. He hoped that chewing was not a requirement for all boatwalas.

He arrived at the ghat early, so he sat on a top step

to watch the sun come up and see the other rivermen assemble. He wondered if merely by being put to work on the old man's boat, he was now considered one of them, an official boatwala. He hoped so. In his vision they merited status well above a wide variety of other kinds of workers. He had overheard girls in his village talking about the young, handsome boatwalas and how they sometimes walked the boat ghats just to get a good look at them.

He had been called handsome the previous day. Kabir had no idea how to judge that. Things seemed to be falling into place. Now if he could only learn how to talk to girls.

He spied the old man approaching the small red boat from the north and hurried down the steps to meet him.

"I brought rags."

Upon immediate reflection, it didn't seem like a greeting worthy of the man who was giving him the opportunity to learn the ropes there on the river. He made a second effort.

"It is good to see you, sir."

The old man nodded and spat into the water. Paan, he thought and shuddered. He figured it could do little to pollute the river more than it was. Already that morning, he had seen animal carcasses and perhaps even human remains float by. It was not unusual. There was nothing healthy about the water in the River Ganges and yet by many millions of people around the world, it was revered as one of the holiest places on earth. That surely related to its long believed source from the toe of Vishnu, rather than the quality of its water. Pilgrims came there from hundreds—even thousands—of miles away to bathe in the sacred waters.

The old man took a seat on the bottom step and unfolded the cloth he had carried. Inside was a container of rice and several banana leaves. He arranged two leaves on the stone surface and dipped out a portion of rice onto each one, using his cupped fingers. It was the way Kabir had always known. He indicated which was for Kabir. They ate, mostly in silence. He wasn't like any teacher the boy had ever known. Most of them never stopped talking.

Presently, the old man hitched his head up toward the top of the ghat. There was a small group of well-dressed young people, most likely students on holiday.

"They'll soon come to us right here. Watch."

Kabir watched. The youngsters descended the steps and then moved from boat to boat, beginning with the best ones at the top of the line, coming toward them. Kabir frowned, not understanding.

"Students. They'll not spend a paisa more than they must. We'll get them. You'll see."

He was right. Without even waiting for their question, he announced, "Two hundred rupees. One hour upstream then back. One ten-minute stop of your choice. We'll answer any questions you have along the way."

The students smiled and nodded and began handing over the money. The boat had four seats. The narrowest was in front and sat only one. The rear seat was reserved for the old man and Kabir. The other students shared the middle seats. Kabir hoped the boat didn't sink under all of the weight. He assumed the old man knew what he was doing. It did sink low in the water once all were on board but remained remarkably stable. He figured it was going to be a lot of weight to move with just two paddles.

The day before, he had studied the paddling techniques used by the boatwalas. With hands spread two feet apart along the paddle, it was dipped into the water, blade wide. The blade was then pulled toward the rear. At that point, the blade was turned to the narrow dimension front to back and eased forward, still submerged. The process was then repeated. Few of the men ever removed the paddles from the water. Kabir figured that technique would make it much easier on the shoulders.

Although Kabir had never paddled a boat before, he felt ready. He wound the rags around his hands for protection against blisters. He offered them to the old man for inspection. With one adjustment, he got a nod. The two of them took their seats and the old man sent the boat out into the water by pushing his paddle against the lower step. Kabir's first few strokes were awkward, but he learned the movement quickly. The old man watched with interest.

"Keep in sync with me. If we're not together the boat will not keep to a smooth, straight course. And don't work so hard. Easy does it. Sit up straight or your back will soon be killing you."

Kabir made those adjustments. He already liked the old man's ways. Being out on the water was every bit as wonderful as he thought it would be. He was relieved to find his stomach tolerated the process well and the question about getting sick soon passed. Kabir's inclination was to paddle too fast but he followed the old man's lead. Slow and steady seemed to be the rule. It was amazing to him that so little effort moved the heavily laden boat along at such a remarkable pace. Water obviously made such a job easier than did wheels.

He was pleased to find that he picked up on new things fast—it had been one of the concerns that had kept him awake the night before. He had been a good student while attending school, but once he learned to read and do basic math he saw no future for himself there. They had no books and the teachers' fund of general information seemed very limited when put up against Kabir's questions.

If there was one unpleasant aspect about Kabir's first day at his new career it was the odor of the river, the stench from the steady armada of floating filth and rotting corpses they encountered. He was familiar with bad air but this was different from that of the factory. He couldn't just step outside to find relief. If he was going to get sick, he decided it would be from that rather than the motion of the boat and water. Two of the students held white handkerchiefs over their mouths and noses.

The students mostly chatted among themselves, clearly astonished by much of what they witnessed. They pointed, calling attention to one thing and then another, the huge number of people, the obvious poverty, the unending sounds of prayer, the naked bathers, the brilliant colors where they appeared, the disrepair of the century-old buildings and the magnitude of the ghats themselves and the buildings that rose high above them.

It is said there is no part of the human experience that can't be openly witnessed along the ghats of Varanasi: the miracle of birth and the agony of death; the celebration of youth and the burning pyres of those departed; the cursing of young men and the prayers of the elders; the soiled clothes of the workmen and the clean bodies of the bathers. There are cowards and there are heroes. There are the gentle and the hurtful, the good and the bad, the happy and the sad. Mostly, there is poverty. It is all there to be seen, happening simultaneously, as if viewing a fully uncensored kaleidoscope of life.

"Can we visit a vender's boat?" came the first request.

The old man nodded to the student and scanned the shore. He pointed to a boat with ropes strung between tall poles. Knickknacks hung from them on string. It was moored lengthwise against the lowest, wide stone, step of the ghat just ahead.

"We need to turn. Drag your paddle like this. I will continue to pull with mine and we will make an easy turn toward shore."

Again, Kabir mastered the move with his first try. It had not been until that moment that he had considered the boat might need to be maneuvered. Once they were in line with the vender's boat, he resumed paddling. The old man smiled and nodded. It was the first recognition his work had been given. It was a moment of pride and satisfaction. He returned the smile and nod. He felt a connection, a partnership. It was the first such experience since his mother's death. The feeling rapidly grew into one hinting at security, something that had been missing for him since the terrible night that very same river had torn him from his mother's arms.

When they came to a stop alongside the other boat, the students stood and examined the merchandise. Most of them made a purchase, some several. Kabir was amused at how noisy they were as a group, and at the laughter, the wonderful laughter. Not even he and Omar caused that sort of a din when they were battling the river dragon while at play. Perhaps these students' tendency to chat came from their long association with their overly talkative teachers! They appeared to be having a very good time and that seemed the way it should be. For a moment, he wished he were a part of it, dressed in fine clothes like they were and using words he really didn't understand. That passed. It couldn't be for him. None of them had so much as looked him the eye. He remained the invisible source of power behind their adventure. In every other way, they remained untouched by his presence.

CHAPTER SEVEN

The next morning, he awoke to a body writhing in pain. His arms hurt. His legs hurt. His chest and stomach and backside hurt. Even his fingernails and his scalp throbbed. He had expected some discomfort but nothing so severe or extensive. At that moment, he realized he had a momentous decision to make: Should he actually try to sit up?

He did, of course. It was at the same time excruciating and humorous. There he was feeling like an old man while he was certain the old man was at his own place feeling like a kid. He examined his hands. They had actually weathered the day fairly well. He had worked an application of his mother's salve into them just before he went to sleep, which was, perhaps, three minutes after he had entered his hut. He had been exhausted. They had taken seven loads of tourists. The old man said it had been a very good day.

Kabir did some figuring. From the factory he earned three or four rupees a day. Sari weaving was a time-consuming activity. That came to around fourteen hundred rupees a year. With his share of the two hundred rupees per tour, the amount of money he could earn on the river seemed simply staggering.

There had been no further mention of his wages, although the meals had been substantial. The old man clearly remembered about the appetites of teenage boys. He seemed wise in many ways. Kabir hoped to learn more about him as time went by. He was not a talker, however, and the boy didn't think it was his place to pry.

Another thing had become clear the day before. Tourists made no effort to engage him in conversation. Those wonderful tales about far off places he had hoped to hear remained aloof. To those with such stories, Kabir was merely a strong back—a silent, mostly invisible peasant laborer who existed to serve their needs. He determined there and then that if he ever became rich, he would treat all people with respect.

The bread from the day before had hardened, but it was all he had. He slipped into his long shirt and set off for the boat ghat. He had noticed that many of the boatwalas

—especially the younger ones—worked barechested. He wondered if he should. They, however, had well-muscled chests and shoulders, reflecting physical maturity and years of hard work. By comparison, his body was still more that of a boy. He'd cover up until that changed.

The hour-long trips upstream had taken him just about as far away from home as he had ever been. It all looked the same. He had learned a great deal that first day. When traveling upstream, they kept close to shore, where the oncoming current slowed in the shallows and dropped its debris. The return trip was always easier paddling. The old man directed the boat much farther out toward the middle of the river. There, the water helped push them along. The old man told the tourists it was so they could get the broader view of the banks and the ghats and view the other side of the river in more detail. Kabir suspected something different and always smiled at the old man as they turned around. He winked but never admitted it was anything other than what he said.

The tourists that sought them out, typically comprised of a small group of some kind—friends, family, classmates or fellow workers. They were given to spontaneous conversation and willing to confront one another over controversial matters. Kabir noticed the tourists in the largest boats were mainly quiet, as if strangers, perhaps. He preferred the smaller chatty groups. He listened. He learned. It made the time pass relatively quickly.

During the next few months, Kabir came to feel at home on the boat and with the old man. He learned about patching the leaks and keeping the inside clean and clear of clutter. He learned about the ghats and memorized trivia to tell the tourists. His hands became well calloused and his arms and back grew into the physically demanding challenges of life as a boatwala. He also experienced a growth spurt and the muscles that had evaded him for so long began to find their places. Girls looked at him differently than before. He liked it but hadn't the faintest idea what to do about it.

He always had stories to tell Omar when they could find time to be together. Omar had remained at the factory. He seemed envious of Kabir's improved spirit and new experiences, but his father insisted Omar remain a factory worker. He liked driving the trucks and occasionally making deliveries into the heart of the city. Omar missed his friend, however. As the two of them had determined earlier, things changed. For Omar, that was accompanied with a degree of sadness. Kabir was too busy learning new things and having new experiences to see life as anything but expanding in a grand fashion out before him.

There conversations had changed as well. Girls became a main topic. It was about girls as a breed apart, as objects to be sought out and studied from a distance. It was about girls as females and possible companions. It was about their curves, their lips, their eyes, and smiles. The shy ones, the bold ones, the ones who might actually speak to them.

The boys had listened to older boys speak like that, but now such conversation and thoughts seamlessly crept in. Kabir's shy curiosity became emboldened as he morphed from boy into man. Neither he nor Omar had been properly prepared for their maturation. Sanskruti was the mother and such talks were not her place with her son. There was no father. Omar was the last of seven boys and his father had assumed—mistakenly—they had, at some point, had the discussions. Still, he was, undoubtedly, the more knowledgeable of the two, thanks to his older siblings who were more than willing to share what they knew.

The lives of Kabir and Omar followed pretty much those same paths during the following year, growing taller and stronger. Kabir's work brought him financial prosperity—well, relatively speaking for one of his age and position. However, he and Omar never spoke of money. Omar realized Kabir was doing well. Kabir understood that Omar wasn't and probably never would. Still, they remained friends.

One morning, some ten months after starting with him, the old man led Kabir up the row of boats along the ghat and introduced him to the owner of a large boat—one with its seats arranged around the edge. It was painted and was very wide and deep. Clearly it was designed for an upscale clientele. Kabir figured a boat of that size and width would be difficult to move through the water.

"Deepak, I want you to meet Kabir. He's been with me going on a year. He is strong, dependable, good with people, and not given to annoyance or anger. He is ready to move up to something better. He won't work cheap, but he will be worth every rupee. He gets three good meals a day and will need to have Wednesday mornings off."

Deepak looked Kabir over and motioned for him to turn around.

"You came by here a long time back, right? I remember your features, even more handsome now than then, and you're taller. He's strong, you say? My boat is much harder to move than yours, old man."

"He can handle it."

"Okay, then, I'll give him a week to prove himself. Agreed?"

"Agreed."

It had come as a surprise to Kabir, and he truly didn't understand all that was going on. Clearly the old man was doing his bargaining for him, and doing it well. More money. Three meals. Half a day off. None of it seemed to consider his wishes, but then all of it seemed to consider what was best for him. He would miss the old man but understood it was time to move on. The old man had predicted it that first day.

His pay doubled, but then so did the effort necessary to do a good job. There were more runs a day and some added a half-mile upstream. Again, he was exhausted come darkness, but he adjusted. He missed the old man's flat bread and vegetables, but food was food and there was plenty of it with Deepak. The blades of the paddles were wider and thicker as were the handles. Kabir adjusted. His hands had grown bigger and his arms stronger. He came to like the feel of the new paddles—the way they moved more water. He felt more in command of the river. With that mastery came a sense of freedom and control. These were new and unfamiliar feelings for him, but Kabir adjusted.

Deepak was far stronger and his strokes were longer and more powerful. At the beginning, Kabir struggled to keep the boat on a straight path. It clearly amused Deepak, and he let it be known. Kabir could smile through his struggle, remaining relaxed but focused as he pulled harder and with longer strokes. Before long, he had so mastered the process that, on occasion, he playfully put the strength of Deepak to the test. He never won, but that wasn't really the point. He had bonded with his new employer.

Kabir had never thought of himself as a competitor. With Deepak, it was a requirement. Everything was a contest. His earlier life had not demanded it, and his mother had not encouraged it. It was partly the competition among the top students that had soured him on school. He could have gotten the top scores, but why do that? The idea of being the best just to be the best made no sense to him. School had been an unpleasant place and in many ways a baffling experience.

Even as a boatwala, being the best served no real purpose. The tourists certainly had no way of knowing that and didn't use it as a basis for selecting a boat. He did his job well and was rewarded accordingly. He asked no more from his job or his life.

CHAPTER EIGHT

Kabir's features had matured, partly because of age, but largely because of the harsh life he endured. His straight black hair of youth was now thick and wavy. His brown eyes still conveyed a solace visible to others, if not to himself. The muscles in his shoulders and arms, although thin and sinewy, were strong. He was growing rapidly and more often than not, his trousers only reached his shin, leaving his ankles bare. His exposed shins and baggy trousers accentuated his lean build and narrow waist. Generally, he carried a carefree and happy expression. His dark-bronze skin handsomely outlined the whiteness of his eyes and teeth, and when he smiled, it had a most alluring effect on others.

The tragedies in his life had left a gaping cavity in his soul, which became a receptacle for compassion. His longing for intimacy grew. It seemed to compel him to seek out the company of the young women in the village. His brotherly love for Omar was loyal and deep, but his heart yearned for another dimension of love. At that point, it belonged to no one.

The final years he had spent in the factory allowed satisfying fantasies about reunions with his father and mother while he worked at the loom. They had become like reliable friends. But they hadn't moved him forward. His vivid imagination was little more than a wellspring for unrealized dreams.

That had changed. His boyhood fantasies had been replaced with images of him flirting with girls and conversing with his vision of the perfect beauty. He imagined himself caressing her fragile fingers in the long palms of his hand and tenderly stroking her hair, enthralled in endless conversation with complete attention both given and received. He even dreamed about how her kiss might feel—soft youthful lips pressed gently against his, their arms wrapped in a tender embrace. Trust, tenderness, and affection, these were the things he knew were missing from his life, and his unquenchable, unrequited impulse to seek out the company of girls continually reminded him of that. He was reminded as he saw the girls walking along to tops of the ghats. He was reminded by the silhouettes of the women sitting ahead of him in the boat, between him and the bright reflection of the River Ganges. He was reminded as he passed groups of giggling girls in the marketplace and on the paths and streets of his village.

His early life had been one of childish simplicity and innocence. There had been little overt affection displayed during his upbringing—hugs from his mother and an occasional kiss. Sexual innuendo had escaped him. In the end, his growing understanding of love and affection would necessarily emerge along the natural path of self-discovery as he traversed the steady, if hit-and-miss, journey from innocence to manhood. There had been no models, right or wrong. There had been no media, so often tilted to distort genuine lovemaking into a contrived version of lust and selfish passion. He was on his own to explore, evaluate, and render his own findings. Perhaps that was all in his best interest.

Kabir came to realize that up to that point in his life, he had never overtly reacted to the flirtatious stares from the local girls. He had seen them, just hadn't done anything about them. Things had changed, and recently he found himself deliberately seeking out opportunities to encounter what he characterized as small groups of youthful beauties as they made their way to and from the market. He became proficient in smiling at them and making eye contact, but this was not enough—he wanted to engage them in conversation, and draw them into his life. How was that to come about?

His inexperience with such kinds of social interaction left him with many questions, so he again turned to the one thing, which had seldom failed him—his imagination. The most probably successful scenario was to make himself as conspicuous as possible, standing on the sidewalk where they were sure to travel or in the doorways of shops girls his age frequented.

There was a prominent gravel intersection where three roads converged. A side road became a large sweeping curve as it merged with Main Street. The sidewalk there was broad and left plenty of room to engage girls in conversation, should his plan succeed. And unlike all the other corners, which turned at right angles, the sidewalk along a nearby street would allow him to see them coming from a distance and continue to provide him a clear view as they passed.

His plan was set for Wednesday morning. He awoke early and groomed his hair with an actual comb, a purchase he had made with recent earnings. He decided against eating his morsel of bread but rather to take it with him so he would have something to do other than just stand there waiting. The girls usually strolled to town just after the second call for prayer.

So Kabir left in time to arrive just ahead of them. He arrived before the heavy traffic set in. When he reached the spot—he had determined it would best allow him to put his plan into action—he felt a surge of awkwardness. A taxi rolled to a stop to see if he needed a ride. He laughed at the absurd thought of himself ever riding in a taxi, with nowhere to go.

Relax, he told himself, wondering just how a young man his age went about doing that. He thought it might be best to be casually leaning against the wall when they arrived. His empty stomach gurgled so loudly, he was certain it had been heard throughout the market. He decided he should get that under control by eating some of the bread. Before he realized it, he had nearly devoured his best and only prop. Leaning felt unnatural. Nobody was leaning. He began pacing back and forth. Realizing he had no useful plan of attack, he averted his eyes to the sidewalk, trying to think of what he could say to get their attention without sounding foolish. How was he to know what girls might think sounded foolish? Clearly he had not put enough thought into the activity. It was to be much more than just finding the perfect place and position to appropriately showcase himself.

Ready to move on and go back to the drawing board, he looked up, surprised to see a group of six of girls, about his same age, walking his way. They were draped in brightly colored clothes of orange, pink, and saffron. There, against the dusty road and weathered brown buildings, he thought they resembled a bouquet of flowers. Each wore a colorful shawl, attractively draped around their shoulders. Some were sheer and others opaque. All appeared to be silk. Dressed as they were, Kabir figured they were probably out of his reach. That did not keep him from looking.

The girl that most caught his eye was wearing a fuchsia gauze scarf. She was slightly taller than the others and carried herself well. As far as he could tell, they had not looked in his direction. They drew closer. Determined to engage them, Kabir fretted over what he might say. As they came still closer, he saw their eyes were indeed upon him. More or less casually, he moved into position in the middle of the sidewalk. They were still too far away to speak to, so he launched one of his wonderful smiles in their direction. Most of the girls sheepishly lowered their eyes. The taller girl did not, however, and their eyes met. Kabir swallowed hard. His mouth went dry. He needed to clear his throat but thought that might seem crude and out of place, so he continued to smile through his distress.

He managed a pleasant, “Hello,” offered through a faint crack in his voice.

“Hello. Are you doing well?” she replied.

It seemed almost too forward to Kabir, but then he had no idea what to expect.

He was relieved and encouraged that she offered a question. It was like an invitation to continue the conversation. It could have been much less, he thought—a single word, merely being polite for example, or even none at all, which would have been a flat-out, devastating snub.

He was sure she could see the wild thumping of his heart through his T-shirt. It was from the previous summer, so he feared it was perhaps too tight.

It seemed to be his turn to speak. He couldn't just let this opportunity end so quickly. He mustered the courage to say, "Would you mind if I walked you to the market?" He was amazed at his forwardness and nearly choked, wishing he could recall the words.

She paused and graciously crossed her arms. She looked him over and nodded.

"Yes, that would be fine ... nice, even."

He felt encouraged. He felt terrified. Where should he walk? Should he stay behind the group or move in beside her specifically? Was he just with her or with all of them? Thankfully, the girls were well ahead of him and paired off, allowing him room next to her. It couldn't have been better if it had been a planned maneuver, he thought.

They walked along together. *Walking* he knew how to do. It was the *talking* about which he was uncertain. She made it easy and soon they were conversing. An hour later, he wouldn't remember what had been said, but they were still engaged in conversation. He, Kabir, was walking and talking with an attractive young lady. As hard as it was for him to believe, there he was, a tall, lanky, barefoot boy surrounded by a bouquet of beautiful flowers. From time to time, his talking stumbled over his smile.

They managed to linger together for twenty minutes or

so.

“We must go on now,” she said at last, referring to herself and her friends.

“Can I see you again?” Kabir asked, again surprised at his own forwardness.

“I’m here every week at this time.”

It seemed like another clear invitation to Kabir.

During the next seven days, his all-consuming focus was singular.

As a boy, he had accompanied his mother along that very sidewalk hundreds of times. He remembered it differently. There was an ever-present bustle of people hurrying off in all directions as the two of them walked to and from the factory through the market. Those had been the short moments of dawn and sunset. It was the hour of the day that made the difference. During the late morning hours, a more businesslike calm settled over the area. Shoppers took their time. Merchants waited patiently. Kabir preferred the slower tempo of midday. He decided to see if Omar was free for a swim or a chat or a tussle before he returned to the boat. He had things to tell.

Omar was a willing listener. Kabir babbled on about her hair, her cheeks, her clothes, the easy conversation, and, of course, her lips—seen though not touched. Omar had a similar tale to relate but it would wait for another day. He would never spoil such an important moment in his dear friend’s life.

CHAPTER NINE

Her name was Arundhati. Kabir thought it was the most beautiful name he had ever heard. Arundhati. Arundhati. Arundhati. He said it over and over. The next Wednesday morning, there were only two other girls. How fortunate, he thought. After a minute of small talk, the others left. Arundhati and Kabir spent several hours together. They walked. They sat together on the low stone wall beside the grocer's shop. They talked and laughed. Kabir presented her with a candy stick—an expensive present for so early in a relationship, he thought, but it was worth it.

During the next weeks and months they met often. He spent time at her home—far larger and more pleasant than his own but still a hovel. Her family was also Hindu. That was important to Kabir. He had vowed not to live a repeat of what his father and mother—and as a result, he—had to endure.

Some days she would bring the noonday meal to him at the ghat. He had to endure the teasing of the other men, but Kabir wore it as a badge of honor, proof of his emerging manhood. She found work with a novelty vender, a boat that sold the knickknacks so popular with tourists. Between her beauty and her easy way with people, she did well and her employer gave her a raise. It was nowhere near what Kabir was earning, but then she lived at home and had her family for support.

Mostly, she just liked the excuse to be close to Kabir and to watch and brag about him as he moved the big boat in and out of the ghat. She and her friends thought he was handsome. She liked his gentle ways and his eagerness to learn. She knew many things he didn't. He had many questions for her about those things. Books, politics, even sports. Her family had several books and let him read them.

They remained modest—private—about the romantic side of their relationship. They never kissed or caressed in public. Handholding was sufficient. They agreed romance should be a personal thing just between them. These times alone were wonderful, even more wonderful than Kabir had envisioned and certainly different from the boyhood fantasies he and Omar had conjured.

With a girl in his life, Kabir came to understand that even at his current pay level of two hundred rupees a week, he would find it difficult to support a family. His hut would never do for someone so used to better things. He learned that women's clothing was expensive. A pair of sandals could cost a month's worth of work. Deepak related how difficult it was to support his own growing family even on the amount of money he earned as the owner of the boat. Making a living with his back and shoulders would be a hard and spare life. Kabir longed to continue his education but believed that opportunity had passed. Young men worked or young men went to school. Both could not be, and he had nobody to support him.

His benefactor continued to leave food for him several times a week. At one point, Kabir thought he should pretend sleep so he could find out who it was. Upon thinking it through, however, he decided against it. That person clearly wanted to remain unknown to him, and he should respect that. Still, he sometimes wondered about it and considered contacting several sources in the village, but never pursued it. Kabir chose to believe that for some reason he was special to somebody else and that made him feel special to himself. Life was far better when he felt special. When the time came that he would be financially able to do the same for a needy youngster, he would continue the tradition.

Kabir came to detect an unsettling feeling within himself. It was true that many things were going well— the job, Arundhati, his continuing relationship with Omar, and several new friends among the boatwalas. But he had come to understand, once a boatwala, always a boatwala. He felt that he was being squeezed into a mold that might not be best for him. He questioned whether or not the river should be his calling in life. It meant always living in poverty—toward the higher end of poverty, perhaps, but poverty nonetheless. That was all he had known, and he had accepted it as his lot, but seeing people in nice clothing who were able to pay for tours and spend lots of money at the venders' boats had stirred ripples of dissatisfaction inside of him. He overheard the tourists talking about their lives in the cities and even in foreign countries. He heard about train and airplane rides and cruises in huge ocean-going vessels.

Kabir concluded that life had been happier before the unsettling had come upon him. He had been more content and less apt to be dissatisfied. He had always accepted whatever he had with thanks and a glad heart. But recently, that was being sorely tested. He had no idea what he wanted, so he could have no idea how to obtain it. It was not something he thought he should talk about with Arundhati—she was a woman and not to be worried about such things—and Omar just wouldn't understand.

One Saturday morning, he arrived at the boat to find vandals had damaged it. Deepak and the carpenter from the village were already making repairs. Kabir offered to stay and help for no pay but was sent him away instead.

"Too many hands will just slow down the process. Go. Have a good day," Deepak said.

Tours would continue the following day. The carpenter had called him by name. It seemed odd, but then many people in the shops had come to know him since it was where he and Arundhati spent much of their time together. Such recognition felt good. He returned a nod and a smile, even if baffled about hearing a supposedly mute man speaking to him. For most of his life, Kabir had been a nobody, not even known among the other nobodies. Someone simply knowing his name infused his self-esteem.

Arundhati would soon be at work. His plan was to walk back up the path toward her place, meet her, and walk her back to the ghat. They might even kiss in the dim light of early morning as well.

After delivering her to her boat, he left and walked back to the area of shops in his village. It was hard to decide what to do with an entire day to himself. As he passed close by the stall where jasmine flowers were available weekends, Kabir noticed a face out of his past. He couldn't place who it was, but that face was unforgettable. It belonged to a large elderly man dressed in a white suit. He wore a large gold watch on his left wrist and in his right hand he held a cigarette, carried in an ornate ivory holder. He reeked of money, success, and class and was accompanied by a servant. It was that steady stare that he launched into the world that Kabir remembered.

A servant whispered to the big man. He stepped forward.

“Kabir?” he asked in a strong, deep voice.

Kabir was taken aback, being singled out by name like that. The man, familiar as his face seemed, was a stranger. Perhaps he should just continue on his way, as if he had not heard. His inquisitive nature would just not allow that.

“Huh?” Kabir managed, turning his head and taking a closer look. It was then he realized this was the same peculiar looking man he had seen right there years before, the quiet man with the piercing gaze. Kabir took a step in the man’s direction. His servant whispered something close to his ear. Suddenly it became clear. The old man was blind. His servant functioned as his eyes.

“Kabir?” he repeated. “I am your grandfather.”

The boy stood speechless.

It could have been true. The goatee, the large frame, the deep, resonate voice. Blindness, however, had never been mentioned. It could have happened more recently, of course. The age seemed to be about right. But such a fine appearance. Surely that would not adorn any of his relatives. Why would he be there? How would he have been able to just pick him out right off the street like that? Clearly, he hadn’t. It had been his servant’s eyes, but still. Perhaps he had heard of his mother’s death. Why had he been there years before? Had he returned often, perhaps to spy on him? The questions kept coming, questions Kabir had never before had reason to contemplate. What if he were his *father's* father? He didn't even want to begin thinking about the multitude of problems that could unleash.

The old man spoke again.

"May we talk son? In the teahouse, perhaps. Do you like tea?"

Kabir shrugged, immediately realizing it was a futile gesture since the old man could not see. His servant whispered, again, and again the old man spoke.

"Please. Just give me a few minutes of your time."

"I suppose, but I have lots of questions."

"Good. Good. I like young men who are filled with questions."

"They are all about you, sir."

"Even those will be welcomed. You should have questions. I assume I will have the answers you seek."

Kabir found the old gentleman unexpectedly easy to talk with. He quickly grew to like him. The man presented himself as his mother's father, an assertion Kabir would have to confirm on his own.

As they sipped tea, the old man said he had been blinded in an automobile accident many years before. That was when Kishan became his personal assistant.

"But automobiles and personal assistants and white suits and ivory things to hold cigarettes—those things must be very expensive, sir. I can't believe my grandfather could have that kind of money."

"Your mother's name was Sanskruti. Your father was a Muslim named Shahid. He was from north of the city. They never married. They settled here in this village away from both of their families so the families would not have to live in the shadow of their shame."

"I'm thinking I am that shame, right?"

The old man cleared his throat and continued, choosing not to restate or confirm the obvious.

"So, let's say you are my grandfather. What's your name? Where do you live? Why are you here?"

"Slow down. All in good time. How about a pastry with the tea? Boys your age are always hungry."

"I've never had a pastry. Probably wouldn't like it."

The old man turned toward Kishan and nodded. The servant rose and went to the counter.

The old man continued.

"My name is Virat Chowdary. I am seventy-two years old. I have been told that my white hair and beard make me look older. I have lived most of my adult life in New Delhi, where I am a lawyer and earn a very good living."

Kishan returned with a pastry for Kabir. He wasn't sure how to go about eating it. He looked around the room for hints. Just pick it up and chomp, he concluded. He hesitated. Kishan again spoke into the old man's ear.

"Just try a small nibble. I'm sure you will like it. If not, just let it be."

Kabir picked it up and sampled a nibble. His face lit up, and he tried more. It was the most delicious food he had ever eaten. Kishan maintained a running, whispered play-by-play commentary for the old man, who also smiled.

"Good, yes? I knew you would like it."

"Yes, sir. Thank you, sir. It is wonderful. Thank you."

He was babbling on.

They talked for the better part of an hour. In the end, Kabir believed the old man's story. His grandfather had found him. What was to come next remained unclear, and Kabir was determined not to make hasty decisions. It was just more than he could assimilate.

"I need time to let all of this soak in, sir."

"Will you come and stay with me at the hotel in the city where I have a suite? It's the Suryauday Haveli—best in the Varanasi."

Just to say the hotel's name seemed important to the man, as if it made him in some way more important. Kabir let that be. He had never been inside a hotel and didn't understand what his grandfather meant by the term "sweet."

"I can't do that. I must be at work at dawn."

"You don't seem to understand what is going on here, son. You don't have to work now. I want to take care of you. I want you to return with me to New Delhi and live there with me. We will work out the details as we go, as we get to know one another."

"Oh, sir, thank you, but I don't think I could ever do that. This is my home. I have my hut. I have a very good job as a boatwala and I have a girlfriend. She is Hindu, if you are wondering. I have Omar, my best friend from childhood, and several new friends from the boats. I have even put back a small savings."

The man paused, stoking his beard. "I see. Well, then, can we at least meet here tomorrow at this same time to talk further? I really do want to get to know you better. It is like I have found a long lost gem."

Being referred to as a gem was certainly a good thing. No one in the village had probably ever before been referred to in that way. Gem wasn't even a part of the day-to-day vocabulary there in his land of small huts and narrow passages.

"That will not be possible, either. I must be at the boat by sunrise. We missed a day's work today due to vandalism, so we will need to do extra tours."

Clearly the boy was not getting the message.

"After work then. Here."

"The teahouse will be closed by the time I could get here."

The man was not one to be bettered. He again nodded at Kishan, who again got up and went to engage the owner in a short conversation. He handed something to the owner. Kabir could not see what. The owner came to the table and bowed politely.

"It will be my pleasure to remain open late tomorrow so you and your grandfather can eat, drink, and talk."

The old man paid him off, Kabir thought. Who has enough money to do that?

"So?" his grandfather asked.

"So, okay, I suppose. I'll be here shortly after sunset, but I can't stay long. Work the next day, you understand."

"Whatever you say."

Kabir heard the words but wasn't convinced that *whatever you say* was how it would ever really be with this man.

CHAPTER TEN

Options. Kabir had really never had options—not truly life-changing kinds of options like he was being offered. He had thought them through. He felt he could trust that the man was his grandfather. That would make him the only known relative in his life. He felt he could trust that the invitation to go live with him in New Delhi was genuine. Why else would it have been offered? He had traveled a great distance to seek him out, and the trip must have cost a great deal of money. He certainly had no reason not to believe the man was wealthy. After leaving the teahouse, he had hidden across the street to watch them leave. Kishan left first and returned driving a car—not riding in a taxi but driving a car. That had to mean money. He pondered over and over why his grandfather wanted him and why now. If Kabir was truly a gem, then why had his grandfather waited so long to seek him out?

Kabir had sometimes dreamed of having lots of money, but in these dreams, lots of money meant having a clean long shirt for every day of the week and moving into a two-room hut with a real door and glass window. It meant that, were his mother alive, he'd be able to buy her three beautiful dresses and allow her to work fewer hours at the factory. This had been his vision of wealth. But this thing with his grandfather was as different as the small pond behind the factory was to the mighty Ganges.

He walked aimlessly for many hours. In the end, he found himself sitting beside the factory pond as if it were an old friend. It had always been a good thinking spot. It was where he and Omar dreamed their dreams together as boys and arrived at their own, if often not fully accurate, answers to the mysteries of the universe. Omar was out making a deliver, which was good. Kabir needed to be alone with his thoughts and seeing his old friend would make his decision more difficult.

He understood what staying in his village meant for a man's future—long hours, hard work, little pay—so he didn't dwell on that. It was the possibilities posed by his grandfather that needed his exploration and evaluation. City life and his grandfather's way of living would be foreign to him. Both his grandfather and Kishan wore shoes and stockings, for example. Kabir had never worn shoes—never even slipped his feet into a pair. The men smelled good. Men in his village and at the river reeked. Although the heart of Varanasi, a huge city, was only miles away, he had very little experience there. His several delivery trips had been as much frightening as exciting. He was always relieved to get back to the village. There was so much chaos in the city, and he felt certain he could not get used to that. He would feel like a grain of rice simmering all alone in a full pot of water.

It was also a very noisy place—cars honking, trucks and buses passing by with their huge engines roaring, the din of voices as people made their way along the sidewalks. All these things were intimidating and solid reasons to stay put.

There was another side to it all, however. He was sure the city offered more possibilities—possibilities for a better job, mixing with people who would have wonderful experiences to relate, new things to see and places to go. With a better job would come more money and the possibilities that could bring; never having to be hungry was the first thing that came to mind. Kabir's mother had always provided well, but *well* in the village did not mean always having a full stomach.

He wondered if he would have to wear suits like his grandfather and Kishan. He was quite certain he would not like that. He needed to have that next meeting to hear about how life would be—what his grandfather's expectations would be of him. It would be possible to move there with the idea of just trying it out, even if he were never to come right out and state that. If it was not to his liking he could always return, perhaps on one of the large passenger boats that ran the Ganges. He wondered how he and his grandfather would travel to New Delhi. Surely not in that car. Maybe, though. He could help drive. That would be fun.

It would mean leaving his friends—Omar, Arundhati, Deepak, the other boatwalas he had grown close to. Most of all, though, it would mean leaving Arundhati. He had already determined that although he liked her very much and really enjoyed being with her, especially being alone with her, he really didn't love her. He was not fully sure how love felt but was sure it involved more than just liking, having easy conversation, and occasionally kissing. He thought about the way in which his mother had spoken of his father. The look on her face and the tone in her voice suggested something far greater than what he had with Arundhati. Couples broke up all the time. Surely he could find a way to do that too. He wouldn't want to hurt her, but he wasn't about to marry to avoid the hurt. Perhaps he could sell it as just a separation until he worked things out. Perhaps there was just too much untruth in that. He would figure something out if he decided to leave. Suddenly, it sounded to him like he needed to figure something out about things with her whether he left or not.

Kabir lay back in the grass to think some more. He was soon asleep.

The next day on the river, he remained preoccupied. Several times, Deepak had to remind him about things he hadn't had to mention since the first week he had been on the boat. Deepak understood something big was happening in the boy's life but didn't press any further than keeping him on track.

In the evening, he would often wait for Arundhati and walk home with her. That night, he took off on a trot, by then eager to explore the possibilities that had been dangled in front of him. He felt his grandfather was not one to wait around for others to make up their minds. As the day had worn on, excitement swelled. It was an excitement about possibilities he knew could never be his there on the ghats. He had been satisfying himself vicariously through the stories told by the tourists. Suddenly, it appeared that he just might be on the cusp of living those stories.

It was frightening to think of leaving everything he had known, everything that had provided his sense of belonging and security. In the village, he knew what others expected of him. He knew without any doubt what was right and what was wrong, what was good and what was bad. He wondered if these things would be the same with his grandfather in New Delhi. He wondered about bigotry and prejudice in the city. It had been an all-encompassing part of his daily life for as far back as he could remember. He was not merely Kabir. He was not just the friendly kid next door. He was not just the boy who wove at the factory. He was first and foremost the bastard from the mixed religion parents. He wouldn't dwell on it or make it the main basis of his decision, but contemplating leaving all that behind loomed large in his hopes for a better life.

The two men were inside the teahouse, sipping tea at the same table as the day before. As Kabir approached, Kishan raised his hand and snapped his fingers in the direction of the shopkeeper. His tea arrived as he took a seat.

"Good to see you both," Kabir began, looking from one to the other.

"And you," his grandfather replied with a smile.

It hadn't been a really warm, inviting smile, but perhaps lawyers didn't smile that way.

"I've been thinking about what you said almost every minute since we talked yesterday," he said, raising his cup and blowing on the steaming tea.

"I'm sure you have questions," his grandfather said.

"I have so many its hard to know where to begin."

Without hesitation, Kabir fired off strings of questions that his grandfather patiently fielded one at a time. After more than an hour, Kabir was spent, already exhausted from a long day paddling on the river. Now his mind was fatigued. The night's sleep to prepare him for the following workday had become fully unimportant.

At one point, he all quite inadvertently eyed the pastry counter. It wasn't his way of asking, he just looked in that direction. Kishan again snapped his fingers and a pastry arrived.

"Thank you, sir."

The comment had been directed at Kishan, although he was sure the man was only carrying out some understanding between the two of them. His grandfather couldn't see, so Kabir assumed the focus of his acknowledgment was irrelevant.

"Let me sum up," the grandfather said at last, as if playing out some climactic courtroom drama. "You will live with me in my home in New Delhi. You will attend a private school—the best. You may have some say in which one after visiting several. I will give you an allowance each week, buy you new clothes, provide transportation as required, hire a tutor if needed, and in general, take care of all your needs."

Kabir responded with silence. He looked into the man's face. The man allowed it as if looking back. Kabir didn't flinch. The exchange was not unpleasant, just very direct and matter of fact. It was more of a getting to know one another—an exploration of just what sort of relationship could come of it.

Kabir had one final question. It was the most important, and yet he had no idea how to judge the quality or sincerity of the response. He asked it anyway.

"Why?"

It elicited another smile from his grandfather. All his smiles looked the same, so they provided little help in understanding the man.

"You are my grandson. You are now alone. It is my place to care for you. I want to do that. I want to give you the life my grandson deserves. I want to be able to be proud of you."

It had not contained the main element that Kabir had been listening for—that his grandfather loved him. Perhaps it was too soon in their relationship for that. Kabir realized that he could not honestly say he loved his grandfather either. He shouldn't expect to receive it if he couldn't give it. He put the omission aside.

"When would all of this begin?" Kabir asked, at last allowing the possibility to move toward the next step."

"Immediately. Tomorrow at the latest. I am needed back in New Delhi."

Somehow, in that instant, it seemed more about his grandfather than about him. Perhaps that was just his way —the businesslike way of the big city lawyer. Perhaps Kabir really didn't want to believe that possibility, so he put it aside also.

"How would we travel?" he asked.

"By train. First class, the air-conditioned class. It is the best there is. We will have a sleeping compartment to ourselves—the four of us. It is nearly a twelve-hour trip.

We will leave at eight on the Varanasi Delhi Special and arrive at ten the following morning."

He already had it planned. It would give Kabir most of the next day to get things in order. They could all be accomplished in that amount of time. His heart raced while he drew deep within his being to make his decision.

"Okay then. Thank you. I will be honored to go to live with you in New Delhi."

Kabir seemed more surprised at the answer than his grandfather.

"Do you have much to pack? Do you need luggage?'

They had again been very businesslike questions focusing on process, not relationship.

Kabir thought for a moment. The loom was in poor shape, and he would leave it behind. He had a picture of his mother drawn for her by a neighbor woman. He had two shawls she had woven. He wouldn't need his pots and pans. He could carry the few rupees he had stashed under the rock in his floor in his trousers. He had but one pair of trousers and one long shirt. He would be wearing them, as he was at that moment, of course.

After taking that mental inventory, he repeated it aloud.

"A small valise, then," his grandfather said, turning toward Kishan.

The man whispered to Kabir's grandfather.

"Kishan indicates that you will need clothes for travel. When we pick you up, we will provide what you need."

Kabir nodded, granting to himself that it had probably been a valid observation.

"Thank you. I am so grateful. I hope you understand that."

His grandfather nodded but spoke no words. Kabir began to think that words of appreciation and emotion might not be a part of the man's personality. His grand presence did offer an immediate sense of security, however. He understood that he would be safe and well taken care of.

"You mentioned four of us?"

"We three and my secretary, Rishi."

"Is there food on the train, or should I bring some?"

"I have arranged catering. Train food is generally disgusting."

They decided where and when to meet. Kabir was to have his things out in front of the teahouse at that time. Kabir felt there should be some shaking of hands or a hug or some rite to seal the arrangement. None was offered, and the boy thought it would be out of place for him to initiate such a thing.

They stood.

"I look forward to meeting you here tomorrow, then."

It had been Kabir speaking.

He left the building and took off on the trot for his hut. What was to become of the hut? It was sad to think of giving up the only home he had ever known. The neighbor man to the north was sitting outside, smoking. Kabir informed him that he would be leaving the next afternoon and asked him to find new residents for his hut.

Inside, he gathered the things he would be taking and wrapped them in the larger of the two shawls. He would leave his bedroll and cooking things for the new residents. He counted the money he had saved. It came to just over three hundred rupees. It was a source of pride for him. His mother had never had savings. He tied the money in a rag and put it with the rest of his things. His mother's one silk scarf hung on a peg. It was not something he needed, but it was something he wanted. He folded it and kissed it and added it to his things.

He lay down knowing he would never get to sleep. There were just too many things to think about, too many wonders, too many possibilities, too many things to get done the next morning. How surprised he was when he awoke to the songs and flutter of the birds.

CHAPTER ELEVEN

Kabir's first duty was to tell Deepak that he was leaving. He was sure Deepak would be able to find a replacement that very morning. Deepak's boat was one of the finest moored at that ghat. There was both a new supply of bread awaiting him and a pastry he had saved from the night before. The operator of the teahouse had bought him two pastries with his tea. He had never imagined anyone might have more than one pastry at a sitting. He felt like his good life had already begun.

He left his hut with the piece of bread in one hand and the pastry in the other. He couldn't decide which to eat first, so he went back and forth between them. He set a fast pace as if that would somehow bring Deepak to the ghat earlier than usual. He sat on the top step and finished his food, watching the sun come up over the river, especially when morning clouds hung low on the horizon. Their underbellies were painted with an ever-changing wash of wonderful hues, from the faintest pinks, through fuchsia, to multiple shades of red and orange. It was reflected below on the smooth surface of the water as if setting the whole world ablaze. Omar said that to appreciate such a thing was not manly, but Kabir noticed his friend would also watch in wonder at such celestial displays.

Deepak did arrive early, and Kabir descended the steps two at a time to meet him.

"Get the boat fixed okay?" he asked, thinking it would be a good conversation opener.

"Better than new. The carpenter knows his stuff. Didn't have time to paint it. The patch is right at the water line. Should have painted it. Now it will be wet and will stay too wet to paint. Not sure what I'll do about that.

"Just tell people its like a scar acquired through its years of fighting the Ganges, and that it wears it proudly," Kabir suggested.

"Not bad. May use that. Not bad at all. Hungry?

"Not really. Ate on my way this morning. Had leftovers. I need to talk with you."

"Sounds serious."

"It is. The most important kind of serious."

"You dying, boy?"

"No. Well, sort of, I guess in what I'm hoping will be a good way."

Deepak was clearly confused. He laid out a meal for himself as they sat turned toward each other on one of the lower steps.

"My grandfather came for me. He lives in New Delhi. He wants me to go and live there with him. He seems to be rich. He says I can go to school there and have an allowance and lots of things that sound really good. I hate to give you such short notice, but it all just came up and he has to get back to work. He's a lawyer."

"Lawyers do make lots of money. And school. You are a smart boy. You should go to school. I am very happy for you."

It had been easier than Kabir thought. Nothing the man said really surprised him. It had been good to have his smart side confirmed by him. Kabir had grown to like and respect Deepak.

Kabir stood.

"Well, I guess this is goodbye, then. Thank you for ... well, for everything. You have been kind and a good teacher. Best, I guess you have been a good friend."

"I know you'll do well. One piece of advice: Once you leave here, don't come back. It's like a trap here. We are born inside the trap, and we can never get out. Stay away."

Kabir nodded into his friend's face. It was returned. Kabir left, walking north along the ghat down the line of boats to visit Red. He had kept in contact with the old man. It was never much more than stopping by and saying good morning. The old man would offer rice. Kabir would shake his head and say Deepak had food waiting. They would nod at each other, and Kabir would leave. It meant more to both of them then any observer might think.

That morning began as a repeat of their ritual. Then Kabir broke the news. The old man's face lit up in a way the boy had never seen before. It left no doubt that he was happy for the boy. They exchanged nods. Kabir felt sad. He turned and ran the steps to the top.

He walked the path that Arundhati followed in the morning. He practiced what he would say. Goodbyes were different with girls than men. Men nodded, patted you on your back, and it was done. Girls cried and clung and said they didn't understand. Men made you believe it was okay. Girls made you feel guilty or sad—probably both. He couldn't seem to make up a speech that he thought would properly serve the occasion. He'd just have to let it happen as it would happen.

Her face brightened naturally as she saw him round the curve in front of her. He forced a smile and bit at his lower lip. The closer he got, the more difficult he knew it was going to be. She reached out for his hand. He accepted it. They walked together. He was glad she hadn't tried for a kiss. He didn't know why, but it felt better without one.

"I got some news to tell you, and it may make you sad."

Arundhati frowned and turned her head toward him.

"What? Are you ill?"

He wondered why everybody thought his was sick.

"No. I am fine. It is my grandfather."

"Your grandfather is ill? I didn't even know you had a grandfather."

"No. He is not ill. Yes, I have one. I didn't know where he was until a few days ago. He is from New Delhi, and he wants me to go live with him there."

"And you are going, of course. That is the news that will make me sad?"

"Yes. I'm sorry. But yes. I leave today."

After a moment of silence, she spoke.

"You'll never come back, you know. We'll never see each other again."

She began to sob. Kabir couldn't decide if putting his arm around her would help or make things worse. She stopped walking and turned to him, pressing her head against his chest. He held her. He patted her back. He couldn't find any more words. It went on in silence that way for some time. She eased back and wiped at her eyes and cheeks with the backs of her hands. Kabir offered his shirttail. She smiled into his face.

"I am happy for you, Kabir. You should have more than our village or the river will ever be able to offer you. Mother and father have said so to me. In lots of ways, we have grown up together. These will be memories I will always treasure. I'll never forget you, you know."

She brushed back his hair with her soft hand and kissed him on his forehead.

"Thank you for our time together. I'll just walk on by myself now."

She turned back to the path and moved on. Kabir remained behind. He wiped a single tear from his cheek. She had said all the right words. He started toward the factory.

It was still early and no one would be there for another fifteen minutes or so. The doors would be locked, but he and Omar had long before discovered a way in where siding boards swung loose. He entered and surveyed the room. It didn't seem as large as it had when he was a little boy. He walked to what had been his mother's, and later his, loom. New warp had been strung, ready to receive the colorful threads that would create a new shawl or sari or scarf that day. He sat on the stool and thoughtfully passed the empty shuttle back and forth several times. He stood and kissed the frame where his mother's right hand had so often rested, ready to catch the shuttle and send it back in the other direction. He left the way he had entered. There was no looking back.

He waited by the pond, tossing in pebbles and watching the ripples live out their short lives as they traveled to the bank. Omar would arrive soon. That was how it was. He did. A huge smile burst across his face when he saw his friend sitting there. He ran to meet him. Kabir was not going to linger over that goodbye either. There would be no reminiscing, no relating of the good times or the scrapes they got into together. They already carried those memories.

Kabir said his say. Omar's smile faded momentarily but was soon coaxed to return. He was happy for his friend —just sad for himself. He was grateful for their years of friendship. He would miss him greatly but sometime before, they had recognized together that change was to be a part of their lives.

None of that was said, of course. They were men. Kabir stood, and Omar followed him to his feet. They managed an embrace—no one was there to see. With awkward, unpracticed pats to their backs, they separated. Kabir turned and walked back to the street and headed home. Of all the goodbyes that morning, that one had been the hardest. The two of them had really never had anything important in common. One a Hindu and one a Muslim. One a bastard and the other from a family of many children. They were friends because they shared years at the factory. They became united because of a common enemy, Malik. One had attended school for several years. The other had no formal education. Kabir had taught Omar to read. He hadn't really taken to it. They had tested their childhood mettle against one another, and both had grown because of it. It truly had been the most difficult of the partings.

The train would leave from Varanasi Junction, a huge railway complex north of the city. It would be a several hour journey by car from the village. He just had time to pick up his belongings and meet his grandfather. He had timed things well.

Kabir tried not to think about things like these last times he saw the important people in his life, or that it was the last time he would walk the streets and paths that led from the factory to his hut. He hurried by the secluded spot where he had first kissed Arundhati and the spot where they had said goodbye. He looked at his hands. As a child, they were always stained from the dye vats at the factory or the monkey business at the pond with Omar. As a boatwala, they had become calloused—tough, the way skin turned under the stresses of hard work.

He entered his hut and to his surprise found a small valise waiting for him. He opened it. It contained several things: a new white long shirt made of silk, new black trousers that covered his ankles well, stockings, and black shoes. Changing clothes went well until the shoes. It was a struggle, but he figured them out and stood up in them for the first time. What a strange feeling. He made sure he had salve because he was certain they would rub his feet raw.

He put his belongings into the valise and snapped it closed. He left his old shirt and trousers on the floor. He was sure somebody would find and wear them. It was, perhaps, the first time he had ever abandoned anything that still had useful days left in it. It felt strange—unrighteous, even. He had effectively said his goodbye to the hut the night before so, valise in hand, he ducked through the door for the last time and headed toward the shops. He would just be able to reach the teahouse at the time his grandfather had specified.

For a moment, he wondered if he might be making his way through some sort of dream. When would it have begun—while swimming for his life in the Ganges that terrible night, the morning he knew for sure his mother was dead, the day he began work as a boatwala, the morning he had first looked upon Arundhati, the moment he spied the stranger with the familiar face and the piercing stare?

The shoes already hurt his feet beyond belief. Surely, it could not be a dream!

CHAPTER TWELVE

The car, with Kishan standing beside it, was waiting out front when Kabir arrived at the market. He could see his grandfather and another man in the back seat—the secretary, Kabir assumed. As he approached the vehicle, Kishan stepped to the rear and opened the trunk. He took the valise and set it beside three larger pieces of luggage.

Kishan directed Kabir to sit in the front seat, and then took his place behind the steering wheel. As they pulled away, Kabir turned to face the men in the back.

"Good morning, Baba."

It was the first time he had referred to the man in that way. It felt odd and yet comfortable.

"Good morning, Kabir."

He turned his head, indicating the man sitting beside him.

"Rishi, this is my grandson, Kabir."

"Good to meet you. I see the clothes fit you well."

"Yes, sir. You are the one who purchased them, then? Thank you. I have never had such fine things to wear. I'm not sure if I feel out of place in them or if they feel out of place on me."

It had been an odd thing to say, and he hoped his intention had been understood.

Rishi smiled broadly and chuckled. The others remained stoic. Kabir immediately liked Rishi. He was younger than the others—he guessed mid-thirties. He had slicked back black hair and bright brown eyes. His features were pleasant. Like the others, he wore a suit, but unlike the others, something about him said comfortable, easy, playful. If he were going to be required to wear suits, which seemed to be the case, he would try for Rishi's style.

Of the three, Rishi was the one who kept the conversation going. He seemed genuinely interested in learning about Kabir, who was accommodating. Kabir relaxed in his presence and easily rolled out his life's story. If there were just the two of them there, he would have provided more details. Perhaps that had been his grandfather's plan—have the younger man become the friendly inquisitor so he could learn about him.

Kabir was not entirely sure what a secretary did—well

other than buy clothes, wear comfortable suits, travel with his employer, and take the lead in conversations. He was sure he would find out more in the coming hours and days.

The ride took them through areas that were new to Kabir. He was fascinated by what he saw—clean streets, individual houses, parks with green grass. The further they traveled away from the river, the fewer barechested men and boys he saw. He would have to ask about that later. It was, he surmised, only the first of many differences in lifestyle ways he would need to learn. That was exciting and, at the same time, frightening. Most of all, he was convinced it was going to be good for him.

He had always been a fast learner—in school, at the factory using the loom, in the vat rooms, and on the boats. He had learned to drive the truck in just a few minutes, just as he had paddling. He also quickly grasped how to cope with new people and relationships. He saw no reason that he shouldn't be able to catch on to the different ways of his grandfather's world as well.

The railway station was huge. Kabir couldn't figure out how Kishan knew where to go among the maze of streets and buildings. They parked the car, secured their luggage from the trunk, and walked to one of many stations. Inside, Rishi approached a window. Behind it was a man wearing a cap with a stubby, shiny black bill. A few minutes later, he returned to the group with instructions as to where they needed to go. It was a huge, open room with hundreds of benches and many of the kinds of windows Rishi had used.

There were more people in that room than Kabir had ever seen in one place before, and the gatherings on the ghats for evening prayers were huge. Many were well dressed, like him. How interesting. There were military people bedecked in uniforms with braid and medals. He had to wonder at all the interesting stories they would have to tell.

Rishi pointed to a door. Beyond it was a dock and beyond that on the track, a magnificent, shiny silver train with bold stripes in brilliant colors. It contained a long line of cars pulled by several engines. It was amazing. Rishi went up to a conductor and showed him the tickets. They were ushered aboard. The workers inside seemed to know the three men. Kabir assumed they must have taken the train regularly. They were escorted down a narrow passage lined with bunks on one side—called berths by the attendant—and windows on the other. Between the berths were doors opposite the windows. The attendant stopped in front of one, opened it, and entered ahead of them. They followed.

"Is this satisfactory?" he asked, directing his question to his grandfather.

"Yes. Quite. There will be a caterer along."

Rishi unfolded several bills into the man's hand. He bowed slightly and left, closing the door. Then, he turned the latch to lock it.

Kabir stood wide-eyed. It was a not a large room, but

what a room it was! On the front and back walls were seats below with a berth above each. The berths were made up with sheets and quilts and pillows. He wondered how the four of them would sleep with just two narrow berths. Perhaps they would take turns sitting and sleeping. He would not mind sleeping on the floor. It was carpeted. Rishi understood the question on the boy's face. He showed him how the seats converted into lower berths.

The room was cool, and Kabir investigated the cold breeze flowing from a slotted opening near the ceiling.

"An air conditioner, just for me? " he said, amazed.

Along the outer side, opposite the door, were windows covered in drapes that matched the quilts in color and style. He had never dreamed of such a place. Even with the three men it provided the most privacy he had ever known —not that privacy was in the least important to him. Rishi and Kishan stowed the luggage under the seats, and his grandfather sat down.

"So, what do you think of our accommodations, Kabir?" he asked.

"Accommodations, sir?"

"This place. The seats, the beds, this compartment, as it is called."

"It is beyond words. The trains I'm used to have people riding on the tops of the cars and hanging onto the front and sides."

"Sit," Rishi said at last, patting the surface beside him.

"Try out the seats."

Kabir sat. He ran his hand across the heavy fabric that covered them. He bounced ever so slightly and felt the give—the spring—and smiled. It seemed humorous to him. The whole experience brought a run of nervous chuckles.

"A meal will be along shortly," his grandfather said. "Once we get underway."

The old man felt the face of his wristwatch, one clearly made for blind people.

"That should only be a few minutes now."

He was right. The train jerked slightly and eased ahead. Kabir moved the drape aside with his hand and looked outside watching the world begin to roll by. Some of the nearest sights began to blur as the train picked up speed. He heard the sound of the wheels on the track. They clicked along, faster and faster. He had never moved so rapidly, and at first it was a bit frightening. Eventually, he came to relax and enjoy the view.

Rishi and Kishan marveled at the boy's ever-changing expression and his comments, which indicated complete ignorance of such experiences. Perhaps naivety would be a better descriptor than ignorance, although where one concept left off and the other began was often impossible to discern. He looked, he bounced, he smiled, and he ran his shoes across the carpet.

"Perhaps you want to remove your shoes, son," Rishi said. "When a guy's not used to them it can be uncomfortable."

"Thank you. Yes, I would very much like to remove them ... and the stockings too?"

"Sure. The stockings too."

Removing them seemed as difficult as putting them on had been. The deed was soon accomplished.

"That does feel much better. Thank you."

Rishi leaned down and looked at Kabir's feet. There were large open blisters on his heels and along both sides.

"Perhaps you got shoes that were too small. I had to guess. We need to care for those blisters."

He took a small box from his briefcase. It contained bandages. They were unfamiliar to Kabir. Rishi showed him how to peel off the protective paper and apply them. Kabir took over after one demonstration. He smelled them.

"Nice," he said and then continued to attend to his problems.

The men were amused but privately had to admit that bandages do smell nice.

They ate. They slept. They awakened.

All quite magically, Kabir thought, there was a car waiting for them when they climbed down from the train in Delhi. It was like no car he had ever seen, much longer and newer than the one they drove in to the train station: extra long, shiny black, a window between the driver's seat and the rear of the vehicle. The backseat was where back-seats should be, but the rest were arranged in a semicircle facing it. There was room for a dozen passengers. He could have easily lived in there. It was larger than his hut. More amazing, yet, his grandfather owned it.

The drive back into New Delhi took another hour. It was a beautiful city—at least the part he saw. Old buildings, new buildings, tall buildings, not so tall buildings, stone and brick buildings, and most amazing of all to Kabir, buildings of glass. Eventually they passed out of the business section and into an area filled with houses—the biggest houses Kabir had ever seen. The car pulled into a circular drive. There was a black iron fence with matching gates that reached nearly twelve feet. The gates opened magically and let the car pass through. It was a magnificent house of two stories and perhaps a dozen rooms. He wondered which of the rooms belonged to his grandfather. He figured a man of his apparent wealth would have more than one.

He asked.

"They all do. This is your grandfather's house. Now, it is your house too."

He figured it was large enough to house all the boatwalas who worked from his ghat plus all the families of those who worked in the marketplace and the sari factory.

"You must have many grandchildren to need such a large house."

"No. Just you," his grandfather said.

There was a pompous tone to the remark, but that escaped the boy.

It seemed like a sinful waste of space, but he wouldn't say it out loud.

"See the corner room on the upper floor, right there?" Rishi asked, pointing.

Kabir nodded.

"It is your room. I will take you to it."

A room all of his own. How strange. How lonely. How wasteful. Clearly these were not the thoughts his grandfather assumed he would have in response to it all.

The car stopped and more servants approached them. Two took the luggage. One held the car door. Another held the front door to the house. One handed Kishan several notes. He scanned them and whispered to the boy's grandfather. It was most likely about business, Kabir decided.

Inside the front door, Kabir picked up the valise that contained his belongings, and he followed Rishi up the long, wide staircase. The room that was to be his sat just to the left of the top of the stairs. He continued on ahead and opened the door. It appeared to be higher off the ground than any tree he had ever climbed.

Kabir dropped the valise and just stood there, dumbfounded. There were four very tall windows across the front and three along the side. Each had brilliant white sheer curtains across them and drapes along each side. Rishi showed Kabir how to pull a chord that closed and opened them. Why one would close them, he didn't immediately understand. The ceiling was almost as tall as the front gate. Distributed across the hardwood floors were rugs of beautiful colors and wonderful designs. In the front corner was a bed like no bed he had ever dreamed of. It was clearly wide enough to sleep five and so long he would not be able to touch the top and bottom at the same time, even with his arms extended above his head. It had a tall post on each corner and, of all things, a roof overhead. There were four pillows and silk sheets and a striped bedspread in blues and browns. It matched the drapes. Rishi showed him several closets and his private bathroom, complete with a porcelain bathtub, then he demonstrated how to turn the water on and off.

"A place to bathe," he said, just to make sure the boy understood.

He pointed out the soap and washcloth and, in a motion, demonstrated their use.

In the outside rear corner of the bedroom was a sitting area with a couch, two chairs, a desk, and a case filled with books. A long, narrow black box sat on its own small table.

"A television set," Rishi explained.

Kabir walked close and looked at his reflection in the screen.

"Very nice."

"Tomorrow we will go shopping and get you clothes. We will be sure they are your size. Like I said, I had to guess about what I got you earlier."

"But I have clothes. Like you said, they fit fine."

“Here you will need several outfits. I will explain another time. On the dresser is a watch. You will need to wear it because here in the city, time is important. We will eat the noon meal in one hour. Come downstairs at that time, and I’ll show you the dining room. After we finish, I’ll take you on the grand tour.”

Kabir furrowed his brow.

“I’ll show you around the house.”

Kabir nodded. He was simply overwhelmed. No one had thought to prepare him. It was hard for the men to imagine how little knowledge of their world a youngster his age could have.

“May I suggest you try out the bathtub before you come downstairs. I think you will like it. Use the washcloth and soap like I showed you,” Rishi said, demonstrating again. “It will leave your body clean and smelling wonderful.”

Kabir nodded. Rishi left.

The cool bath did feel wonderful. He worried just a bit about coming out smelling like a girl, but he had noticed the other men smelled good, so he suspected it was the way things were in the city. The process intrigued him enough that he actually removed much of the grime that had become a part of his body over the years. Next time, he would be more careful with the soap on his face so his eyes would not burn from it.

As he dried himself with the largest towel he had ever seen, he looked out a front window. There were many other large houses in the area. The streets were wide and there were lawns of grass with ancient trees. Sidewalks paralleled the streets. He had been transported into a fantasyland. Perhaps that was more of the dream that had begun sometime before.

He sat on the edge of his bed, pulling on his trousers and stockings. He assumed shoes were required in the house. Until told differently, he would wear them. He wanted to do like his grandfather expected, and he really had nothing to go on. He needed to have a long conversation with Rishi.

He wondered what his mother would think if she could see him there among all the wealth and finery. Suddenly, his three hundred rupees seemed insignificant. He would keep them safe as a reminder of his earlier life. He also wondered if early in her life, she had lived in that house. When the time seemed right, he would ask, but not his grandfather, because he had clearly disowned her. Perhaps Rishi would have the information.

The meal was wonderful. There were dishes he had never had before, but he tried every one of them. He concluded he would be able to adjust to the food with no problem. Remembering to use the silverware was going to be another matter. A sweet dish was served last. He especially looked forward to a repeat of that one.

He was exhausted that night, but could not get comfortable in the bed, so he took a pillow to the floor and was soon asleep.

CHAPTER THIRTEEN

Rishi found Kabir on the floor the following morning.

"Time to get up," he said, opening the drapes, which Kabir had closed in order to sleep. He was not used to the constant bright light that the city offered at night.

Kabir was astonished and a bit ashamed that he had slept so long. The night on the train had been uncomfortable. There was also the nervous exhaustion that accompanied the rapid transition from village life and his hut, to city life and his castle.

"Problem with the bed?" Rishi asked with a smile.

"It's so soft, like the ground was rolling around beneath me when I tried to sleep. No offense, you understand. Things are just so different here—not bad, I tell myself—

just different. Well, the shoes I would have to classify as bad."

They shared a knowing chuckle.

"We'll go to a special shoe store today where I know a man who will be able to fit you with a perfect pair. You'll feel like you're walking on air.

Sleeping on a mattress that moved beneath him was bad enough. He felt sure that walking on air would be no better, but he smiled. He stood and pointed to a long white garment at the foot of his bed.

"Is that what I am to wear today?"

Rishi chuckled.

"No, actually that is a sleeping gown. I failed to tell you about that."

Again. it seemed like an extravagance. Why would you need to wear anything while you were sleeping? The unnecessary outlay of money he had witnessed during the previous two days would feed many dozens of people for a full year back in his village. It was hard to understand.

"I found six books on the desk. Do they mean something special?" Kabir asked, slipping into his new long silk shirt.

"They are books your grandfather wants you to read before he takes you for your interviews at schools. He believes they will give you information that will be helpful as you answer the questions you will be asked."

"Questions?"

"The best private schools only accept the smartest and

best-educated young men. The information will be useful for you to know."

"I thought the reason for going to school was to get an education. I didn't understand you had to be educated first. It makes no sense."

"Most of the boys who apply will have been in school since they were five. You haven't had that privilege, so you have some catching up to do."

"I've been reading, and Arundhati, my friend back in the village, shared with me what she had learned in school. I think I know a lot of things."

"I imagine you do. I think you will enjoy the books. Give them a try."

"Yes, sir. I didn't mean I wouldn't. I've always thought books were a privilege. There are more books here in this room—my room—than I've seen in all my life. When I was in school, we didn't have books. The teachers just talked mostly, and we did our words and numbers with sticks in the sand."

They visited two stores. One was filled with rack upon rack of clothes. Together they picked out a dozen outfits. Again, extravagance, Kabir thought. Who could possibly need a dozen sets of clothes? He would surely grow out of them before he wore them out. Then to the shoe store. Rishi had been right. The man there seemed to know everything about feet and shoes. First, he suggested wearing two thin stockings until his feet began feeling comfortable. That would help prevent blisters. Then he slipped Kabir's foot into what must have been the softest, most comfortable shoes in all of India. He stood and took several steps back and forth.

"I can probably stand these pretty good," he said.

The comment amused the men. Kabir wasn't sure why, but he smiled and chuckled along with them. Before they left, he had a brown pair, a black pair, and a pair with white canvas tops and thick red rubber soles. He liked them the best and asked if he could wear them out of the store. Rishi nodded and Kabir was overjoyed.

Right then and there, he decided it was best that he never see Omar again because his friend would never believe the tales he would have to tell.

"We have two months to get you ready for school," his grandfather said as they sat eating the noon meal after he and Rishi had returned. "Every day you will spend time out in the city at museums and such. Every day you will spend the afternoons reading the books in your room. There will be time for fun as well. You will need to discuss that with Rishi. I may secure a tutor to guide you through all of it. We'll see how things go."

"Oh, Rishi is doing just fine, sir."

"But Rishi is my secretary, and he is needed up in my office. He keeps my business running smoothly and with him here with you, things are sliding there."

Kabir shot a sad glance at Rishi. It was returned and

genuine in all respects, the boy thought. Again, things seemed to be more about his grandfather than Kabir. He understood, but he was growing to dislike it.

In the car that morning, Kabir had the chance to ask many of the questions bouncing around in his mind. He learned that his grandfather had a law firm that employed a dozen other lawyers who did most of the work. He also owned an interest in several other businesses, the exact nature of which escaped Kabir. He was somehow involved in politics and government. Kabir knew very little about either and was sure he would not even be able to say what politics was if asked.

His overall impression was that his grandfather was both a very busy and a very important man. It really didn't surprise him—the man had an imposing presence and a take charge manner. Kabir hoped he could live up to the man's expectations.

His questions about his grandmother were glossed over. She had died many years before. The end. It was clearly a topic that was not to be brought up.

After the noon meal, Rishi accompanied Kabir to his room, where they hung up his many purchases on hangers and put things such as stockings and underpants in the chest drawers. Kabir thought the whole concept of underpants was hilarious.

"Pants under pants?"

He let it go at that, just hoping he wouldn't forget to

wear them. Of course, nobody would ever know if he didn't. So, again, why wear them?

After four hours on his feet, the new shoes began to feel comfortable, or at the very least bearable. He wondered if, in this new life, the calluses on his feet would get soft. He hoped not. They had always been a part of him like his hair and nose and knees. He would not be himself without them.

"Which day of the week am I to use the bathtub?" he asked at one point.

"Every day. You may choose morning or night. If you get especially dirty at play, you will need to bathe again before the next meal."

"It seems like a waste of the precious, clean water. Where does it stay before it comes out the handle in the tub and sink?"

"Those handles are called faucets, and it stays in huge tanks waiting for us to use."

Kabir spent the rest of the afternoon with the books. Rishi had been right. They were wonderful. One was about the history and geography of India and nearby countries. One was about world geography. He had heard the world was round and the round maps of the land and the oceans, which seemed to prove that, fascinated him. One was more like a schoolbook. It was about math and started with the regular stuff he already knew and then went on to things he'd never heard about—geometry, algebra and trigonometry. He liked these words, geometry and trigonometry. Just saying them brought a smile to his face.

After several hours with them, he confirmed for himself that he must be a good reader. He made a list of the words he didn't know. There were only a few. Later, when Rishi checked in on him, he asked about them. He took a thick red-backed book from the shelf and explained about the dictionary and how to use it.

"Wonderful! Thank you."

Rishi smiled and put his hand on Kabir's shoulder.

"You know, I'd rather be doing things with you than working in your grandfather's stuffy office."

"I wish you could. Will the tutor be a nice man?"

"I imagine he will, but you have to understand your grandfather tends to be all business. He will go for good academic credentials before a pleasant manner."

Kabir nodded rather emphatically.

"I do understand that. He's great, and I am more appreciative of what he is doing for me than I will ever be able to express, but he seems short on warmth, you know?"

"Believe me. I know!"

They exchanged broad smiles. That moment sealed a bond.

"Tell me more about him and what you called politics."

"Well, let's see. Elected officials run the government. To get elected you need to convince the citizens to vote for you. Politics is what goes on to get you elected."

"You would be a good tutor."

"Thank you. Clearly you are going to be a good student."

"So is grandfather an elected official?"

"No. But he works hard to get the people elected that he wants to have running the city and the country. He donates money for advertising and getting the word out about them."

"What does he get in return?"

"Let me revise my earlier observation. You are going to be an outstanding student. I can't say a lot about it. Your grandfather keeps that all pretty private. Usually, though, men who make big donations get certain things they want, like laws passed that favor their businesses."

"So donating to a person seeking to be elected is like a bribe."

Rishi laughed out loud. "That is never something to utter aloud in this household, my friend. I'd suggest you just spend time listening and observing. There will be a lot for you to learn about him and how he operates. He does usually get his way—here in the house, here in New Delhi, and here in this country."

"Really powerful, then!"

"Yes. Really!"

CHAPTER FOURTEEN

The next several months passed quickly. Kabir visited museums. At the National Museum of India, there were endless paintings and other works of art from India and other countries around the world. The Crafts Museum displayed thousands of handcrafted items made in India. Craftsmen worked right there demonstrating their skills. Kabir was drawn to the woman working on a loom, finishing a sari. He engaged her in conversation and she even let him set in a few lines of thread. Both she and Rishi were impressed. They returned to that museum numerous times.

The National Rail Museum had hundreds of working model trains that told the story of rail travel in India. It was one of Kabir's favorite places.

There were many more. After each such outing, Kabir would hold forth during the noon meal, delighting his grandfather with his knowledge and his enthusiasm. It was the one time Kabir could feel a real connection with the old man. It seemed he was genuinely proud of him, which was important to Kabir.

It became clear that his grandfather wanted Kabir to excel at sports—cricket, field hockey, and football were his favorites. Kabir was mostly unfamiliar with them. His experience with sports was pretty much limited to Gilli Danda, a sport played with a long and short stick. It was a cross between baseball and cricket. The small stick was struck with the long one and fielders tried to catch it. He and Omar played it with pick-up equipment—two carefully selected sticks that fit the bill just for the game at hand. He knew about football and cricket, but there had been no good balls in his village. He had been introduced to football by one of his boatwala friends who had a ball, but they had not had much time to play.

Kabir became more or less comfortable with the new setting—the house, the clothes, the studies, the food, the sports, and even the bed, baths, and shoes. He missed having friends and people his age to talk with but figured that would happen eventually when he entered school. Sometimes when he was alone,he longed for Arundhati but figured there would eventually be a new girl in his life—

perhaps lots of new girls.

The one thing his grandfather did with him was teach him how to play chess. He said it was one of India's great gifts to the world. He picked it up fast, although he never came close to beating his grandfather. He was amazed how the man kept the ever-changing positions of all the men in mind, considering he had no sight.

The time to go for the interviews at schools had arrived. He was fully surprised that it was his grandfather who accompanied him. The headmasters all seemed to know him, and Kabir soon came to understand that it was to really be more about which school his grandfather would allow the privilege of educating Kabir than whether or not Kabir qualified and would be accepted. It was one of the many things between him and his grandfather over which he had no control. He had accepted that.

Prior to the week of the interviews, his grandfather had taken Kabir aside and made several requests of him—demanded several deals *with* him might be more accurate. First, it was not to be revealed that they were related. He said it would be out of place to have to explain about him. Their story would be that he had picked up the boy on a trip to the south and, feeling compassion for him, living as he did as an orphan in poverty, had brought him home to live with him in New Delhi. He was to go to school and do well. Upon graduation, he would be given money for college. He would study government and then law and join him in his firm.

It confirmed for the boy how the man quite skillfully used bribes. To get a college education, he had to play the game. In the back of his mind, however, was his forever option—he could just leave if he didn't like the way things were going. It was his very private option, never spoken of even to Rishi, whom he had come to trust with most everything.

There were far more interviews scheduled than should have been necessary, Kabir thought. Once again, it was all about his grandfather. The headmasters always praised the old man and learned to look upon Kabir as an unfortunate waif suddenly given a real chance in life by this great and generous philanthropist.

Eventually a day school was selected. It was close to the house so his commute each day would be relatively short. It meant more trips to clothing and shoe stores. Students wore uniforms. They were required to be kept neat at all times. Five new outfits were added to his closet.

During the first few months, his school program was individualized. He had his own teacher for much of the day. The purpose seemed to be to determine at what grade level he should be entered into the program. The studies went very well in that setting. When he was transferred into the regular program, however, the atmosphere changed. Many of the boys from wealthy backgrounds looked down on him as an untouchable and were not shy about mentioning it out of earshot of the teachers. The story about his early life seemed to support it, and the stories his grandfather had visited upon the staff further substantiated it. Kabir felt like a ploy for his grandfather, a ruse, or even worse, like one of the pawns he so artfully moved around on the chessboard. For Kabir, the schoolhouse taunting reminded him of his roots and made clear he would never fully be part of the world of the privileged. He may live like them, but he would never be one of them. Not even his grandfather claimed Kabir as one of his own.

A few boys offered friendship. He had never had an abundance of friends so a few seemed encouraging. Much of his free time was spent in study or writing stories in the back of his notebooks anyway. He didn't have much free time to cavort with friends. The curriculum was demanding, although Kabir was up to it even having to come from behind as he did. He played cricket but didn't really like it.

More and more, his grandfather required him to accompany him to events—dinners, political rallies, and other places where his grandfather gave speeches or otherwise excelled as a celebrity. He introduced him to government officials and business executives. Kabir complied, but he always felt put down and out of place. At one such gathering, he overheard parts of a conversation between two of the guests.

"If the boy had been a relative, it would have been his

duty to take him in, of course, but to just take a random waif off the streets of the slums is a wonderfully altruistic thing for him to do."

Kabir began to understand but kept it to himself.

CHAPTER FIFTEEN

The years passed, and what had initially seemed like an exciting adventure, full of opportunities, had turned into a mundane and claustrophobic life. He missed his simple life and longed for companionship. The loneliness and isolation he felt seemed to numb his personality. He spent more and more of his time journaling and writing imaginative stories.

Kabir found a shift in his grandfather's approach to politics. He formed a committee to explore running for office. His grandfather had risen in the political ranks and become preoccupied with his career pursuits, leaving Kabir to himself. On his graduation day, Kabir received his secondary school education diploma alone. What was meant to be a proud moment seemed to feel more like a duty. He was expected to assist his grandfather full time.

As the election neared, Kabir accompanied his grandfather as he traveled the outlying area working to get elected. It meant spending time mingling with his political staff and supporters who Kabir had not really known well before. It allowed him to hear things not meant for his ears.

"The old man wouldn't have a chance without the kid, you know."

"His campaign hasn't released much about the boy. I have to wonder about him."

"We seem to be hearing more about the man's relationship with the kid than we are about what the man stands for."

There were other things that confirmed Kabir's early suspicions that he was being used to further his grandfather's political goals. It had probably been the plan from the beginning. He wondered if he should confront him about it. How would that help anything? He needed that college fund, even though he disliked the dictate that he was to study politics and law.

Kabir had always fashioned himself a very good storyteller. He had grown to love books and desperately wanted to become a writer. He often scribed tales he heard from those around him. There was nothing about politics or law, as it had been demonstrated to him, that held any interest for him. His observation was that lawyers were never required to tell the truth in the defense of their clients, and politicians seemed to feel no compulsion to tell the truth at any time. His mother would never have approved. Truth, honesty, goodness, and helpfulness were important to her. She had never needed to speak of them. Kabir had seen her live her beliefs through her actions.

Then one evening at a local rally, he went outside to get away from the smoke-filled room and the din of the supporters' cheers as speaker after speaker had their say in support of his grandfather. He squatted in the alley, his back against the brick wall. He heard something. Humming. He had heard it before. It was that tune—that mournful tune hummed by the man who had chased them the night his mother died. He stood and moved further into the alley, trying to locate the source. A large man was crouched under a light. The beam illuminated his bald head and faded down his oversized face into his black beard. He had huge hands. Kabir knew who he was. Why would he be there?

He returned inside and found Rishi.

"There is a man out in the alley. He is big, bald, and ugly, with a long, thick black beard. Do you know who he might be?"

"Yes. That's Dev. He sometimes performs services for your grandfather."

"Services?"

"Yes, Kabir. Services. Leave it at that."

The tone of Rishi's voice seemed harsh—something Kabir had never heard from him before. He didn't press.

Things began falling into place. He tried to think like his grandfather. He imagined different scenarios, each deceitful.

It could have begun around two situations, he thought. His daughter—my mother—was a scourge on his family, a disgrace twice over, he pondered. She married a Muslim and had a child—me—out of wedlock. For such offenses many an Indian woman had met her death. The second situation Kabir considered was his grandfather's growing political ambition. He was astute enough to realize that although he had the reputation as the best lawyer in the area, he had not been generally popular. He had successfully defended many unpopular—despised, even—clients. He needed a way to project more humanity and compassion to the public. He wanted to be seen as a family man—an important element for office seekers in these parts. A plan had emerged to encompass both situations. Kill Kabir's mother and rescue the orphan. Then, he could play up the story about lifting an orphan out of poverty, educating him, and giving him the grand new life he continually demonstrated with him by his side.

Such evil plotting, even the possibility of it, made Kabir sick to his stomach. His mother had never allowed hate, but the feeling he had at that moment was full-out, unadulterated, anger-driven hate.

At home that evening, Kabir confronted his grandfather as he sat alone smoking in his den before bedtime.

"I figured a smart boy, like yourself, would one day figure it out. Yes, I sent Dev to dispatch my daughter. Then I watched you mature until I felt you were ready to handle the great change that would be brought into your life when you came to live with me."

Kabir clenched his fists, erupting into a fit of rage.

"I hate you for it!"

It was all he could do to restrain himself from pouncing on the old man. Earlier, he had decided there would be a better way. His grandfather seemed completely surprised at the boy's reaction.

"Hate me? I did you the two biggest favors of your life. I rid you of a terrible woman who brought an indelible shame on our family—mine and yours. I freed you from her, and I have given you this wonderful new chance to make something of yourself."

"I HATE YOU!"

"You don't understand. I only have the highest aspirations for you. I am the one who saved you. Can't you understand that?"

"My instinct is to strangle you where you sit and happily watch the life drain from your contemptible old body. But there is a better way. I have called a reporter from the newspaper and am going to tell him the whole dirty story of what you have done."

"You won't do that. There will be no money for college if you pull such a stunt."

"It is not a stunt. I don't want your money for college. I am sickened to think I have taken your money this long. Goodbye. Keep your humming goon away from me or it will be his life I will take with these strong boatwala hands."

The old man rang a bell, somewhat frantically. It was his signal to summon help. Rishi and Kishan had seen Kabir enter the study. In light of the questions earlier, Rishi was certain of Kabir's intentions. He had shared them with Kishan. They stood outside the door to the den. They ignored the bell and left before Kabir could see them. The boy had put them to shame as well. They, too, had taken the dirty money for too long. That night, the old man's world was to come crashing down around him.

Kabir made good on his threat. The meeting with the reporter was held on the front porch. There had been a leak, and a dozen reporters from papers and television showed up. Kabir told his story. References were supplied who could verify the tale as true. Dev was implicated and the reporter was sure a police investigation would lead to his conviction. The reporter had Kabir sign the notes he had been taking and had it witnessed by his assistant.

Kabir returned to his room for the final time. He retrieved his three hundred rupees, his mother's picture, and her scarf. He gathered some stories he had written. He tied it all into the shawl in which they had arrived.

He laid the watch back on the chest where it had been the day he first entered the room. He slipped out of his shoes and stockings, leaving them on the floor. He donned the simplest pair of trousers and the plainest white long shirt in his closet. He figured his grandfather owed him one thing. He tucked the big red dictionary under his arm and went out into the hall.

CHAPTER SIXTEEN

It was not the way he thought he would be celebrating his eighteenth birthday. He descended the stairs from his room to be met by Rishi. The man handed him an envelope.

"I believe you have one week's allowance coming. There will be no arguing about it. You earned it this evening. I wish you the best and won't ask where you are going. I would never want to let that slip. I treasure our years together. You have taught me many good things about life. I hope that we meet again someday."

Kabir smiled through sudden, unexpected tears. Without a word, he nodded, turned, and left the house. There was only one place for him to go.

He worked his way south, walking, riding in the backs

of trucks, and clinging to the outside of railroad cars. In the early morning hours, a week later, he arrived at his ghat. It was mostly just he and the full moon. He sat on the top step and surveyed the familiar scene—the far shore, the river, the close order line of boats, the steps rising to meet him. It would be hours yet before sunrise. He was very tired from his long trip, so he lay down on his back and slept.

He awoke with a smile. It was the birds. What had at one time been an irritating rush of noise way too early in the day was, that morning, like the sweetest of music. The sun was above the horizon to the east. There were no clouds, so the view was not one of colors blazing, but it was home and that counted for even more.

He watched the ghat come to life. The holy men and the boatwalas arrived. The kiosks that hawked oil lamps and novelties along the river's edge were uncovered, making ready for the tourists. The scene remained much the same, but the people had changed. The red boat was gone along with the old man. This felt like home, but Kabir knew he would not fully return to it. He would wait until later to decide how he would live.

He made his way to the pond behind the sari factory to wait and see if Omar arrived. His schedule had not changed. There he was. He called Omar's name. They ran toward each other and embraced—older, wiser, and no longer embarrassed to show their feelings for each other.

Kabir told as little as possible about his time away. He

told of the train ride and some things about the school, such as football. But mostly he kept the focus on Omar and what had been going on in his life there in the village. Omar was in love. He and one of his brothers had moved out of their family hut and had one of their own, together with a wife. He invited Kabir to stay with them until he worked things out for himself.

Kabir asked about Arundhati. He learned that she spent time with the other boatwala boys but there was nobody special—no long-term friend so far as Omar knew. He confirmed that the old man had died, but there was good news about that as well. The little red boat had been stored and was to be saved for Kabir, should he ever return. It had been the old man's final wish.

"I will take you to it later. Why have you come back?"

"Things didn't work out well. The city was too big and too noisy. I finished school and was ready to come back."

It was both true and false. It was phrased for Omar's benefit rather than intending to represent the whole truth.

"The carpenter asks about you often," Omar said. "I didn't even know you two were friends."

"We weren't. I don't understand."

"I've learned some things you need to know, then," Omar said all quite seriously.

"And those things would be ..."

"You remember the night your mother died. He was the one who pulled you from the water. He had lost a son to the

Ganges many years before, and he said it was like his own boy returning to him that night. He will be so happy to see you. None of us thought you would ever return."

Omar had to get to work. He gave Kabir directions to where the red boat was stashed, not far from the river. They agreed to meet back at the pond when Omar got off work, and he would show him to his new hut.

Kabir was reluctant to be seen. It was less embarrassment than a feeling that he had somehow failed them all. They had been so happy he was escaping the squalor, and disease, and poverty and would be living as an educated man of means. Now he was back where he had started, no better off in many ways. He had seen the privileged world, much of which was distasteful. His boyhood innocence had been squashed.

Because of what Omar had revealed about the carpenter, Kabir decided it was only right to visit him. As he walked and thought, several things seemed to fall into place. It explained why the man knew his name while he was repairing Deepak's boat. It was the carpenter who had secretly dropped off food at Kabir's hut. What a fine man he must be, and Kabir had seldom even acknowledged his existence. He was never rude to him as many of the young people were. He always smiled and nodded when their paths crossed, but he had not gone out of his way to be particularly kind or helpful. Kabir now felt ashamed.

He wondered if he should seek out Arundhati or just let them meet if and when that might happen. He didn't know which would be best, kindest, and most thoughtful. He had broken off the relationship when he left to Delhi as a child. It would be arrogant to think she would want to see him again, let alone rekindle their friendship.

If the old red boat was still water worthy, he could take to the Ganges again and support himself. That was not the life he wanted, but it was a life, perhaps his real lot. But things were different now. He was educated and therefore had more options. What did he want? Perhaps he could teach in the school. Teachers were among the most poorly paid of any of the working villagers. He didn't need much, however. He would need a place to live and wouldn't impose on Omar any longer than necessary. What he really wanted to do was to write. Perhaps he would just write for his own pleasure. That was really what it was all about for him anyway.

As he drew close to the village, its smell elicited so many memories. With only a bit of hesitation, he made his way to the carpenter's shop. He was immediately recognized.

"Kabir! You are back! Let me look at you all grown up. You look well. Are you well?"

His smile wouldn't stop. It had been more words strung together at one time than anyone in the village had ever heard from him.

"I am fine. And you?"

"Much better now that I am looking at you again."

"My friend Omar has related some tales about you—

well, you and me, I suppose is more accurate." Kabir paused, then said, "The incident on the Ganges that night."

The carpenter's smile faded. He became serious as he listened.

"Is it true that you are the one who pulled me from the river and cared for me then returned me to our hut?"

The old man hesitated and sighed.

"It is true."

"Why didn't you tell me? Why did you keep it a secret?"

"I lost my own son to the river. I was afraid if I got close to you I would begin thinking of you as my son, and I dared not replace him in my heart that way. I was still so full of grief at the time. Do you understand?"

"Yes. I think so. It was you who kept me supplied with food after my mother died?"

The words came out as a question.

"Yes. I was so happy to help you, but I didn't want you to think that I thought you couldn't make it on your own. So, I just did a little along."

"You have my greatest thanks ... I am so ashamed, but I do not even know your name. Everyone calls you Carpenter."

"I am Rabindra. I like to be called Carpenter. I carry my tools everywhere I go. I smell like the wood I work with. I am Carpenter."

Kabir sniffed the air. It was the smell of sawdust. It was the smell he remembered from that night at the river. His own senses confirmed the tale of rescue and care.

"What are your plans now that you are back?"

"I haven't decided. The old boatwala who ran the little red boat left it for me when he died. I could begin taking tourists in it."

The Carpenter frowned.

"Why go back to that lifestyle? What are your dreams? Surely you have one?"

Kabir's subdued tone immediately brightened.

"I want to become a writer. I have written lots of stories. I also want to go to university and learn subjects like philosophy."

"And how would you go to a university?"

"That is no longer a possibility for me. I was thinking I can just continue writing for my own pleasure, you know. It is what I love to do so I should just do it, don't you think?"

The old man's eyes danced. Kabir figured it was still about the reunion.

"Kabir, you come back this evening at sunset. We will eat and talk."

Kabir agreed. It was good to have somebody to talk with again.

He left thinking he would just walk the streets and paths for a while. He ended up at the ghat, sitting high on the steps overlooking the novelty boat moored there along the cement dock. He saw her. She didn't see him, but then she was not expecting to see him.

Eventually, he left without contacting her. She was a good memory—perhaps, even, a wonderful and important memory—but what had been is done. That's how he wanted to remember it. A childhood memory. It was trite to say, but they had grown apart.

He walked by the hut that had been his home for so many years. There was a tiny child sitting in the doorway. It seemed appropriate that such a place of love should again be a haven for a young family. Another tear spilled down his cheek.

Back at the market, he bought some flat bread and vegetables that he could eat raw, and he sat on the low rock wall beside the grocer's building and munched. The food tasted familiar—good, in fact. He slept away a large part of the afternoon, needing to recuperate from the arduous days of travel. He needed a bath. He had become used to pure, clean water, scented soap, and privacy. He approached the Ganges. He jumped in the river, like he did so many times as a child, and just floated on his back, reminiscing.

That evening when he returned to the Carpenter's place, he found the lights on and a meal of rice, bread, and vegetables awaiting him. They sat and ate. The carpenter had many questions for Kabir about his past few years. Kabir felt comfortable relating things to him that he had been fully reluctant to share with Omar. The old man hung on every word. He nodded and smiled and continually punctuated the conversation with, "Yes, yes!" and "My, my! and "Go on! Go on!"

Kabir marveled at the immediate connection they made. It was as if the old man had always been a truly important part of his life. For however it had come about, Kabir treasured it and his feelings were clearly mutual.

"I have something to show you," the old man said at last.

He produced a booklet. It told about a college in England. The old man opened it up for him and pointed.

"Writing. See. Classes in writing."

Kabir took some time to look it over. It was wonderful to see, but he had to return himself to reality. It was a boarding program. With tuition, books, and room and board, it came to nearly ten thousand rupees a year. It would take forever to save that much money back on the river. Earlier, he had put that dream to rest. He smiled into the old man's face and began to hand the booklet back.

"No. No. You do not understand. When my son was born, I began saving money from every job I did. It was a fund for his education so he could go and see the world. This place will always be home, but there's nothing wrong with exploring, right? When I lost him, I went right on saving. It has been going on for almost sixty years. There is plenty of money and even some left over if you want to take that fifth year it talks about."

Kabir was stunned. It seemed to be his day for tears.

"It is the kindest gesture I remember having ever

received from anybody other than my mother, but I can't take your savings. You could move to the city and live out your life in comfort."

The old man looked perplexed.

"Why would I want to do that? Move to a strange place and live among strangers? This is my home. It is where I can ply the trade I love. I can stay near the river. It is the only life I have ever known. You spoke earlier of your own difficulties adjusting to the city, and you are still young. Imagine me trying to do that. Bah!"

He pushed his hand in Kabir's direction.

Kabir's mind raced. If he accepted the old man's offer, there would be applications he would have to make and entrance exams he would have to take. He had already taken some of them at the end of his final semester in New Delhi. He could probably use them. His scores were very good. The headmaster said that with them he could go to any university he chose. He reopened the booklet and began reading from the first page. The old man made more tea and watched. It was clearly one of the best days in his long life. He pondered what it might be like to see a foreign country. He was excited but also heartbroken that he would be so far away from his favorite river. Then again, as the carpenter said, this would always be his home.

Acknowledgments

Thank you to Srini Prasanna, Kala Prasanna, S. Rangachar, Radhika Rangachar for their support and encouragement, and to my editor, Joe Coccaro, and publisher, John Koehler.

CPSIA information can be obtained at www.ICGtesting.com
Printed in the USA
BVOW032325240413

319059BV00003B/24/P

9 781938 467387